That Ghoul Ava
Kicks Some Faerie A**

(Book 2 of the critically ignored *That Ghoul Ava* series)

TW Brown

https://www.facebook.com/pages/Author-TW-Brown

Portland, Oregon, USA

ISBN - 978-1-940734-10-1

For my friend Jamie

A moment with the author...

Okay, let me make this clear...Ava is my homage to my favorite decade: The 80s! So, yep, I will probably miss with some of you based on the simple fact that I might "over-use" that gimmick. I am okay with that. If you get all the inside jokes on *Psyche* (one of the USA Network's most under-appreciated shows in my opinion), then you will be fine here.

What I am shooting for here is something light and fun. Something you can read in a sitting or two and not have to think so much. If you smile once or three times, that is great. If you laugh out loud once...excellent!

I have done my homework and read the likes of H.P. Mallory, Rose Pressey, and Barbra Annino among others to see what was out there. Plus, I am a huge fan of Kim Harrison and early Laurell K. Hamilton. (I just sort of lost interest as the Anita story became more about the sex than the monsters.) I think I have something here that is special and will satisfy.

Ava will probably say and do things that annoy you. Is there one single person in your life who doesn't? (If you said yes, you are either lucky or lying.) Sometimes her humor is a bit naughty, and sometimes she will say things that would end a political career because of so-called "insensitivity". I am not out to openly offend anybody, but I won't pull any punches either. I promise to be an equal opportunity offender.

All that being said, I am still trying to develop a character who will experience growth and change. I want Ava to be relatable. I want the people who populate her world to be more than two dimensional extras. I also want to make fun of all of us who love the paranormal/horror genre just a little bit. We do tend to sometimes take our monsters a bit too seriously. Still, if you are reading this and think of the "perfect" Hollywood actor or actress for the part...drop me a line and let me know.

I grew up watching the late night horror movies back in the pre-cable days. And many of you already know my love for the zombie genre. But here is my confession...when I started writing the *DEAD* and *Zomblog* books, I expected a majority of my readers to be a male audience. From most indications, it is the ladies. I'm not saying that the guys are not out there reading my books...but studies show that women read more than men. I wrote this with that audience in mind. Seriously, women are fiercely loyal readers who stick to authors much like men do with sports teams.

So, while I appreciate every single guy that falls in love with Ava, I am doing this with the hopes of commercial success because of you ladies out there who enjoy a bit of fun and humor. You are more likely to tell your friends and share this with your book club. (Although I do sort of cringe for you if you hold this book up and tell the ladies this is your nomination for the month; I doubt I will ever be getting the "Oprah bump".)

Now a word about the chapter titles and the music. Yes, every single title of each chapter is the title of a real 80s song. I even have "Ava's Playlist" on Spotify where I add each and every single song. If you are on that music service and follow that playlist, you will actually see as I add songs because I do it in the moment as I am writing. The funny thing about that is when the chapter goes in a direction different than I intended and I have to change the title (but I still leave the original in the playlist). Oh, and I will also admit that sometimes it might be a bit of a stretch.

More than anything, I just hope that you have fun and can chill out while reading Ava. And now for some thank you stuff and a request: I realize that asking for anything at this point is sort of greedy, but I love reading your reviews (even the negative ones if they are constructive and not simply "Hate" festivals). Getting those reviews on Amazon are a bit of a highlight of my morning as I sit down each day before going to work. I sip my coffee and read them if they are there. Sometimes there are droughts that last days. Believe it or not, your reviews hold power. They move books up in the rankings and make more people aware of them. So, you are actually doing me a favor when you leave one. And that is why I try to at least say thanks each time.

And that brings me to the part where I thank a lot of people you don't know (unless it is your name I am about to mention).

Above all, I thank my wife. Denise never wavers in her belief in me as not only a writer, but also as a husband. I want to thank the lovely and talented Pamela Lorence for being Ava's voice on the audio version. And I apologize for some of the things that I make you read out loud, but also admit that sometimes I write a line with sadistic glee. To all those bands in the 80s that created the soundtrack for my life; to each and every one of you who read my books and let me do what I love for a living; and to all of you who send me an email, letting me know what you think or give me a song that you think absolutely needs to be in Ava's Playlist. Last, but certainly not least, I want to thank my friend Vix Kirkpatrick for being the best Beta Reader (caps are well deserved here) in the world. You rock!

I wanna be a cowboy…and you can be my cowgirl…
TW Brown
October 2013

Contents

1

In the Air Tonight

"Your team!" Lisa said quietly as we walked through the food court of Clackamas Town Center Mall.

"You suck," I muttered, trying not to move my lips.

The 'Your Team' game...is about as politically incorrect as you can get. I am pretty sure that just about everybody will hate me after revealing this...but here it goes. The rules to the game are simple...you see a freaky person of outlandish proportion and you say "Your team" to the person you are walking with.

Now, to clarify...we are not talking about somebody sporting a few extra pounds. These are the people that are well beyond the three hundred pound range on most instances, but often feel the urge to wear Spandex that would squeeze the bony butt of Calista Flockhart and then they go and finish the look with a bare midriff top...belly piercing optional but frequent.

Let me be clear, if you are not walking around at the ridiculous "ideal" weight that some group of demented doctors decided upon...I am right there with you. I am certainly not skinny. I have what I consider a 'Rockin' 80s' sort of bod. In other words, if you go back to your old movie collection and get a good look at say a Helen Hunt in *Girls Just Wanna Have Fun*,

1

or even the first few seasons of *Mad About You,* then you get a good idea of what I mean. Look at her now…scary. She is all lipo-skinny and unnatural looking. And if you are one of those BBW (or BBM) types…you just keep going on with your big, beautiful self. But if you are barely five feet tall and tip the scales at over three hundred…please step away from the halter top.

This particular—I think it is a woman—person is wearing hot pink short shorts that look like a bikini and a shiny, purple polyester top that did not start off as a half shirt. The finishing touch is the 'outie' belly button that would put a few of my ex-boyfriends to shame. And yes…it is pierced.

I was trying not to stare, not that I think my newest team member would care, as we took a seat on the bench at the outer edge of the food court. Lisa and I watched the person stop in front of Cinnabon, purchase a box of six, and then find a table. After the third sticky sweet treat was gone, and number four was about to face the gullet gallows, we decided to get on with the real business at hand.

"You are sure that she said this was the place?" I asked for perhaps the hundredth time.

"I was just as surprised as you," Lisa said with a shrug.

"Morgan and a mall…two things that go together like vinegar and oil."

"Or you and Belinda!" Lisa didn't even try to stifle her laugh.

I stopped at one of the courtyard kiosks that sold useless crap you don't need, but buy anyway. This one was umbrellas. There were ladybugs and skulls and a smiling sunshine. Seriously, the only people in Oregon that carry umbrellas are tourists and the freaking California transplants. Big bunch of sissies.

I picked up one of the baton-shaped wastes of money and turned it over in my hands. This particular version would become a multi-colored rainbow with a white, puffy, smiling cloud on one side and a scowling, droopy, gray one on the other.

"I did not take you for a rainbow sort of woman," a voice whispered in my ear.

Morgan is the regional psychic. She is *not* the fortune teller type. She is more like the mystical "Charlie" from *Charlie's Angels*. She knows every supernatural being in her district and can sometimes offer a job to a ghoul like me. Who knew all that crap you walk by in your bookstore's Urban Fiction section is mostly based on truth?

As a ghoul, I guess I am like the go-fer or clean-up crew. The thing is, almost six months after I became a ghoul, I still am not that much closer to knowing what my purpose is in this world than when I was a divorced waitress barely making enough money to pay rent in my sleazy Southeast Portland apartment and keep my beat up Ford Escort insured. Now I drive a brand new Corvette and have a house in a very well-to-do neighborhood, complete with titanium blinds that keep out the sunlight, and a sound proof basement.

"A bit of a public location to meet, isn't it?" I asked; trying my best not to let on that Morgan had completely surprised me with her arrival.

"Not my first choice," Morgan admitted. "However, you needed to see this for yourself to really understand."

Great, it was time to make Ava feel stupid. I am pretty sure that is one of Morgan's favorite games.

"Oh," Morgan stopped suddenly and spun to face me, "and Lisa must stay here."

"Seriously!" Lisa sulked.

Lisa Jenkins is my best friend. She is completely human. Of course she is in training to become a Templar, but I have no idea what that means since she won't tell me a single thing. Morgan didn't like her at first, but now she treats Lisa better than me most times.

"Despite your new and growing skill set, you would still be at risk, and your commander has already insisted that I keep you back from this mission," Morgan said.

"So I am going solo on this one?" That was actually not so terrible. I love Lisa dearly, but this secrecy thing she has going on as of late has me a little nervous. Something is changing between us.

It reminds me of this friend I had my freshman year in high school. She and I both had a crush on the same boy. The thing was, my friend Kris Dahl was kind of a bookworm. She didn't get out much. I backed off, figuring that I could let her have this one. Six months later she moved to freaking Arizona. You probably already figured it out, but I will share it anyways…

Me and Gary Soderman hooked up. Like every other high school romance (except for this one couple, but I am sure I will get to them later) it flamed hot and fizzled fast. That would have been fine if Kris wouldn't have moved back a year later. We never spoke again once she found out. But back to Morgan…

"I want you to tell me what you see," she said in that normal, emotionless tone she uses. I am pretty sure it would not change one whit if she were on fire.

I looked around and tried to figure out what it was that I should be picking up on. We were on the terrace overlooking the lower level of the mall. I saw people walking. Couples hand-in-hand peeking in store windows and sharing in a laugh. I saw a few of the couples being playful. (By that I mean they were pretty much making out.) Seemed like just another day at the mall.

Still, there had to be something. I dialed up my super seek mode ghoul hearing. Lots of dirty talk! That seemed a bit odd. I bounced from couple to couple…and it was all the same. Then I froze.

Walking down the middle of the concourse was the newest member of my "team" holding hands with a guy that made me just a little bit warm in my tummy. This guy had a chest that could double as a movie screen and arms that showed off enough veins to make a junkie wet themselves.

"What the f—" I started, but Morgan cut me off.

"Tell me what you see," Morgan said in a voice so soft that I doubt she spoke as much as just moved her lips. Hmm, she didn't want to be heard by anybody but me! That was curious.

"The most unlikely couple in history," I said without bothering to lower my voice. What did I care if somebody heard me?

"Faeries," Morgan spoke that one word even quieter if that were possible.

4

"I'd whisper too if I were you." I turned with a scowl. "I realize that you come from an older time, but things have changed and the stigma—" I began my lecture, but Morgan actually put her hand over my mouth.

"No, you foolish girl!" she hissed. "The fey!"

Sometimes I think it is Morgan that is not the sharpest blade in the drawer. I have not been part of the Supernatural community very long. Until recently, I was just like you. I watched *True Blood* on HBO and drooled over Eric Northman like any other gal. Then I found out that he is based on a real vampire. Why is it that Hollywood always casts people that are so-o much better looking than their real life namesakes? Take Diane Downs…child killer. Real Diane—woof! Movie Diane? Farrah Fawcett.

The thing is, there is a lot more truth to your favorite fiction than you might believe. I didn't read much of it before, and I wasn't about to start. My thing was to wait for whatever task Morgan laid out for me, then cram like finals week.

"Fey?" I asked.

"Yes, the fey. Faeries and that sort." Morgan was still keeping her voice to a level that I was certain only I could hear. That meant it probably looked like I was talking to myself.

"Okay, I'll bite," I said, while making an "out with it" gesture with my hands.

"Faeries have a multitude of powers. One of them is sort of where humans got the idea of Cupid."

"So fat little babies shooting arrows that make people fall in love, got it." Seemed fairly simple. I didn't see what all the fuss was about.

"Not quite," Morgan hissed as she grabbed my head and turned it down and to the left.

At first I was dealing with the whole anger thing about being handled so roughly. Then my eyes locked on to a group of young women sitting on a bench in the center of the lower level concourse.

Suddenly, I was like every guy I ever knew. These redheads made me weak in the knees. I wanted nothing more than to roll

5

around on satin sheets with the whole naked bunch of them. That thought popped like a bubble. I was suddenly remembering this one girl from high school named Angela Kersey.

Angela was taller than most of the boys in our class and had this auburn mane that made most of us girls jealous. Not that we would have ever admitted to such a thing back in those days. The thing was, Angela was easily one of the hottest girls in our class, but you never saw her with a guy. She just did her thing. She was nice to anybody and everybody, but you never felt like she was connected to any group. I think she was the first girl I ever wondered what it would be like to kiss. The last I heard— and it was on Facebook so take that for what it is worth—she owned an upscale bar in Orlando, Florida.

"How are they doing it?" I turned to Morgan who was looking at me funny. That usually means that I spaced out on something. Oh well, if she wasn't used to it by now, that was her problem.

"It is something that many have asked, but nobody has been able to answer. Faeries are not known for sharing." Morgan sounded a bit snippy.

"So why don't you go down there and order them to knock it off?" That seemed like a pretty logical question.

"Faeries do not fall under the jurisdiction of a psychic. They have their own hierarchy. The thing is, the Godmother of this area and I have always had a very good arrangement. She is very old school and remembers The Purge…"

I heard the importance behind those two words. I would have to find out later what the hell she was talking about. Yay me for me not derailing the conversation!

"…and she runs a very strict sidhe (it sounded like "shee") with rules expressly forbidding glamour or any sort of human manipulation. This sort of thing can bring trouble."

And that is where I come in, I thought. I was going to have to go down there and bust up this little faerie party. Not the coolest task, but I imagined there would be a catch, a nasty secret that I would end up uncovering by mistake…and a big payday. That last part was really the only thing that I could get

6

excited about.

"Agent Birch reporting for duty," I said with my best effort at standing to attention and snapping off what I thought was a pretty good salute.

"Don't take this lightly, Ava," Morgan warned.

"It is just a bunch of girls having fun," I said with a dismissive wave of my hand. "You simply need to leave it to me."

"I plan on it, but be careful. Their powers are just as potent and effective on most Supernaturals as they are on humans."

"So?" That didn't seem like news. I was obviously incorrect.

"Do you ever wonder why you can't hear me coming, or why vampires smell so unappealing to you? Perhaps you are curious as to why no vampire has bitten you no matter how much they dislike you."

Ouch.

"Not really. I figure it was just the way things are and left it at that."

"It is what humans like to call evolution. The easiest way to explain it to you is that most creatures in the Supernatural community are protected in some way from others. Otherwise we would probably be just as bad as the humans and try to conquer and rule each other in some endless, futile, and destructive cycle. With our relative numbers being so small, it would have led to our extinction centuries ago."

I would have to take her word for it. Personally, I just think vampires are dead things that are past their expiration date. That is why they smell so bad.

"So you are saying I should not simply walk down there and tell them to break it u—" My words just stopped. What I was seeing had left me speechless.

My "team mate" had the super-hot guy pinned to the wall and was kissing him. Hold on…that does not really describe it accurately. It looked like Super Hunk had just told her that a fresh Cinnabon treat was in the back of his throat and she was doing everything she could to get it. Oh yeah, I was now confident enough in my evaluation to call this person a she. Mostly it had to do with the visible thong "whale tail" jutting above the waistband of her hot pink shorts.

"Let's take this to my place," a husky voice said around what I had to assume was an abundance of saliva.

Don't vomit, Ava, don't vomit, Ava, I chanted a few times in my mind. I was not sure that ghouls *could* vomit, but I think I was in the process of being able to confirm or deny that little nugget.

I watched in open-mouthed amazement as Super Hunk and My Team vanished from view holding hands and whispering things that made me regret my super hearing in SO many ways. Now, before you all start calling for my head on a plate, scolding me with tales of lopsided couples, you have to see this pair. Sally Fields was hot and bothered for Burt Reynolds, not Dom DeLuise. And trust me when I tell you, this gal was easily two Doms. Also, hygiene was not something that she seemed to be a big fan of; I can say this because of my super sniffer skill. That, and I did notice a few people turn their heads with a hint of green creeping into their fleshy pallor—ooo, good word, Ava— as she passed by. From what I could smell, I don't think she can quite reach the nether spots after making number two. Also, I think she only put deodorant on one of her three or four armpit folds.

The last thing that I heard before shutting down my eavesdropping on the new Odd Couple was Super Hunk whispering, "When I get you home, I'm gonna—"

Enough of that.

"So this little cupid power…is it irreversible?" I asked, turning to Morgan.

"It can be if whatever chemical reaction responsible for love would have had a chance before the augmentation. However, the spell does weaken over time and can instead cause violent hatred."

"Like OJ and Nicole violent?"

Oh please! Too soon? It has been almost two decades, so don't groan at me. And besides, it was a fairly legitimate question as I would come to discover.

"While not all crimes of passion are the result of faerie manipulation, many can be attributed to it. Some have caused ripples in history. That Helen of Troy mess just about caused the Templars to extinguish the entire species. And before you ask, no, not all people turn to violence, it has to be something in their makeup. (I wasn't even thinking it, but I guess that was a good question.) Trust me, if every one of the couples those little winged troublemakers have bamboozled over the ages committed violent acts of murder...well, let's just say it wouldn't be pretty. Since then, faeries have been more cautious, but this," Morgan waved a hand like the entire mall was some sort of infectious epicenter, "is going to bring some very unwanted attention."

Can I just take a moment to pat myself on the back? One of my readers (who knew I would actually have one...much less dozens) sent me a "Word of the Day" desk calendar. Now, some folks might feel like that was rubbing my lack of vocabulary in my face. I like to think that this person just wanted to be helpful. So, yeah, you read the word "epicenter" and "pallor" in **my** *book. Chantal, my ghost writer, she actually complimented me on my use of multi-syllabic words. Good for me. Okay...back to the mall.*

I leaned on the rail again and looked down at the little gaggle of faerie girls. They all seemed absolutely oblivious to the scene unfolding around them. Also, as I let my gaze wander, sure there were a few obvious mismatches, but with the exception of My Team and Super Hunk, I didn't see anything that might lead to murder. And I thought it would be more likely that Super Hunk would take his own life versus that of what he was going to wake up beside.

"So do I just get them to stop, or do I rough them up?" I asked.

Great. Morgan was gone. As usual, she was sending me into a situation with only part of the information. One of these days I was going to have to really put my foot down. Maybe...probably...some day.

2

Separate Ways (Worlds Apart)

"So what did she want?" Lisa asked as I strolled up in the wake of a couple that were basically feeling each other up while they headed for the exit.

"That I have to be the killjoy for this little grope festival and that—" Something that I can only assume to be "music" began to scream in agony from Lisa's phone.

"Hold on a sec," she said, holding up a finger to silence me much like a mother would a noisy child.

"This is Lisa."

Hmm, that is peculiar, I thought, *I should easily be able to hear what was being said*. My hearing is super sensitive and can pick up whispers from several blocks away, so a person speaking in any tone or volume level on a phone should be no problem. I was not even getting a buzz.

"Uh-huh…yeah…mmm-hmm…okay."

And she stuffed the phone back into her pocket. I stood there for a moment waiting for her to fill me in. She stood there and stared at me with an arched eyebrow.

"You were saying," she prompted, ending our brief stalemate of silence.

"Who was that?"

"Oh…just Templar stuff." Her dismissive wave annoyed me. It wasn't like we had been lifelong friends, but we were still very close. Or at least we had been until the night that she just left and started training to be a Templar. That was another thing that I could blame Morgan for, but at the moment, I wanted some answers.

"So I tell you my stuff, but you keep me in the dark?" I tried very hard not to sound like I was whining. Not sure how effective I was, but I get points for trying.

"You don't have a Code of Secrecy with Morgan."

"And you do with the Templars?"

Lisa nodded. She at least had the decency to look upset. That did not mean that she was going to budge from her silent stance, but at least I could tell that she felt bad.

"Maybe I should go," Lisa said. There was something in her voice that sounded off.

"Yeah…I guess we both have stuff to do. But you rode with me…how are you going to—"

"They sent somebody," Lisa cut me off. "I am supposed to meet them out front of the theater entrance."

I watched her turn and leave…and she did not even say goodbye!. This was becoming a habit, and I was not in the least bit fond of it. She might be training to be a Templar, but that hadn't saved her butt when Belinda came around. The Templars were not the ones that took her home from that seedy hotel…or is it motel…grrr.

Well, it wasn't like I did not have things to do my own self. I was going to tell her that she couldn't come anyways, so…problem solved.

Turning on my heel, I headed up the main level concourse to where I had seen that little flock of troublemakers doing their naughty business. They were about to meet a very grumpy Ava, and trust me, nobody wants to be on the receiving end of that.

I walked past a corridor with the universal symbol for the rest rooms hanging over it and glanced down in time to see three couples practically falling over each other to get inside one room or the other.

"That's just nasty," I grumbled.

I'd had a boyfriend who had suggested on more than one occasion that we slip into one of the stalls at the restaurant where I was waitressing. I didn't mind the occasional back seat hook-up, but I drew the line at a bathroom stall. Seriously, I could barely force myself to use one for its intended purpose, much less try to enjoy a quickie.

Just to reiterate: EWWW!

I passed some sort of candle shop and had to try and not breathe because of how overwhelming the smell from the place was. Now, I am a ghoul with a super-sniffer, but those places have always been a bit much. Anyways, as I passed the place, I see the flock of faeries clustered together. They are pointing and giggling. My eyes track to where they are currently fixated (yay 'Word of the Day' calendar!) and I see this man and woman going at it like rabbits. Seriously, he has her over one of those garbage cans; the kind that is made from various little tan rocks so that they look more "natural" or whatever.

The woman is older, like around her early fifties, but she is that classy sort of pretty. You just know she volunteers at all the visible public functions. Yeah...that type. Super fit, probably does hot yoga and plays tennis every day; the kind of woman that checks her makeup every time she passes a mirror. Oh, and I am not trying to sound snarky, but there has definitely been some work done on the exterior. Sorry, but nobody can be exposed to gravity that long without a little sagging.

One last note; Angelina Jolie's lips look fine on Angelina Jolie. Ladies, enough with the lip plumping thing, you look like you are having a bad reaction to your lipstick...or you just tried to eat a bumblebee.

Now for the man. This is the guy who works on your car. I'm not saying that there is anything wrong with mechanics. Actually, considering my knowledge of a car consists of turning the key and hoping that it makes the 'VROOM, VROOM' sound, I think the world needs those grease monkey types. This guy looks like he just crawled out from under an old Volkswagen with a nasty oil leak. His face has put out an APB on the razor about a week ago, and his beer belly makes it unlikely that he has seen 'the little soldier' in at least a decade. The crowning achievement—please excuse the pun here—is the greasy long lock of dark hair. It has abandoned its position as a comb over and is standing almost straight up; held there no doubt by the accumulated grease after what must be at least three days without having come in contact with shampoo.

So, Tubby is going at it like he has been promised a box of hot, fresh Krispy Kremes and a case of Bud when he finishes, and the porcelain undercover grandmother is howling like Wolfman Jack or Warren Zevon. (And if you don't get the second reference, you have my pity, *Aahh-oooo...Werewolves of London...*I love singing that at the top of my lungs whenever it plays. Note to self: kill and eat Kid Rock out of spite if he uses one more of my 'childhood memory' songs as a loop for his drivel.)

The faeries are all pointing and giggling. I could not actually hold that against them; it was kind of funny to see. If you just take a moment and visualize it, you'll see what I mean. Just picture Sharon Stone and Larry the Cable Guy and you might get the right mental vision.

I had to shake off my own amusement and refocus on the task at hand. Reaching down, I did my best to channel my inner-mother. Steel resolve; check. Straight posture: check. (Hey, don't laugh. How much of an authority figure would I be all slouched over? So, yes...straight posture.) Stern face; check—as long as I ignored the scene playing out about a dozen feet away. Great...he was going faster. *FOCUS, AVA!*

"Hello, girls," I said, gripping my sunglasses by the side and pulling them down to the bridge of my nose. That would give them a good look at my solid black eyes.

"Wow...I haven't seen a ghoul in like...a thousand years," one of the faerie girls squealed.

Excuse me? A thousand years? These girls barely looked Lisa's age. Why do kids always over exaggerate?

"Didn't the Godmother kill the last one?" another piped.

14

Just like that, these girls were all talking at a million miles an hour as they discussed, dismissed, and debated each other's recollection of the last ghoul they had seen. It was starting to give me a headache. I am pretty sure I was *never* like this at their age.

"Okay, enough!" I finally snapped.

Actually, I had to repeat myself about ten times. I am pretty sure the only reason they all went suddenly silent had less to do with me and more to do with the grand finale happening just across the concourse. Tubby actually slid to the floor and now sat with his legs extended, pants around the ankles, and pulled out a pack of cigarettes. Sexy Grandma eased beside him, accepted the proffered stick of cancery goodness, and let him light her up.

"So what brings a ghoul here to the mall?" the first girl returned her attention to me and stepped away from her cohorts. To me, that indicated that I had just found the leader.

"I think it is sort of obvious," I said, opening my arms to encompass the chaotic scene of debauchery (last time, I promise…but just one more, "Yay, calendar!").

"Are you here to kill us?" one of the faeries squeaked.

Whoa, I heard some actual fear in her voice. What the heck was that about? Still, I was seeing some serious changes of expressions on every face but this leader of theirs. Maybe I should play it up a little.

"Not yet." I was keeping it cool. Of course I wasn't here to kill anybody. Was I?

"Perhaps you should stay out of things that don't concern you, *ghoul*." The leader took another step away from her group and closer to me.

I took a moment to take her in, if this was about to get nasty, I wanted to know what I was dealing with.

One of the first things that jumped out, now that I was thinking about her, was the lack of smell. With humans, there is a constant scent coming from them as they all die a little each day. If they are sick, I can actually pick up on that as their death becomes more imminent. A terminal ward would smell like

Thanksgiving is basically what I'm trying to say. This girl—and the others as well—gave off no smell at all. I think Morgan had explained why this was so to me, but I was having trouble with my concentration.

Getting a real good look at her, besides the long, straight red hair that was the color of rubies—so, no, not a natural human shade of red—she had pure white skin without a single freckle, blemish, mole or pimple. In other words, perfect. Her eyes—all their eyes as I let my gaze sweep the group—were an equally unnatural shade of emerald green that not even very expensive contacts would be able to match.

They were all dressed in very tight, revealing clothing that left nothing to the imagination. None had so much as a single piercing, but they each had an intricate tattoo on the left forearm. It was a series of vines with what I was pretty sure had to be runes woven in amongst them.

"Okay, princess," I decided that I could match her in the taking a step closer game, "let's try this again. You are violating a whole bunch of laws here…of both the human *and* the Supernatural variety."

"Name one human law that we are violating," she challenged.

She had me there. I seriously doubted that humans had anything on the books when it came to hexing or spells or whatever it was that faeries do. If I were call 911, what would I report?

"Don't get cute with me, faerie," I growled. I decided that I was going to have to ramp up the attitude with this one.

She reminded me of the rich girls in school. Remember them? The ones who would show up late for class and bat their eyes at the teacher while making some lame excuse? The ones that the principal greeted by name as he passed them in the halls because their mommy and daddy were on some board or another? These were also the ones who had the most insane parties because their houses were so far away from the closest neighbors and the parents were always travelling somewhere on business. Or worse…the parents would be there! You could hear them talking about how it was *okay* for little Constance or Muffy to get plastered, because an adult was present and they were in the "safety" of their own home. These were the kids who would then go to a super expensive college and have the family business dropped in their laps.

Bitches.

"You don't have any idea what you are messing with." The girl actually leaned in so close that our noses touched!

Enough was enough.

"Back off, bitch," I whispered. "I know that what you are doing is going to cause trouble for the entire Supernatural community and I am here to put a stop to it."

"Merriette, let's just go." One of the other girls stepped in, trying to lead away her friend by the elbow.

Merriette jerked away and spun on her pal. "Never touch me without permission, Godiva!"

"Apologies, my mistress," the girl babbled, dropping to her knees and bowing her head in total submission.

"What the—" I started.

"The humans have committed an act of terrorism and must be punished. All previous agreements have been declared void," Merriette said as she returned her attention to me.

"Huh?" I know, not really an eloquent question to such a big statement.

Something that Morgan had said popped up in my mind. I was winging it anyways, so I decided to toss this out and see if it stuck.

"Then should this not be something for the Godmother to address?" I asked.

Yes, I realize that Faerie Godmother sounds cliché, but I didn't make this stuff up. Although it did have me wondering about the possibility of a Tooth Faerie. (I would eventually discover that was nothing to be joked about.)

"The Godmother is dead," Merriette spat. Almost on cue, all the other faerie girls began to weep and moan.

I didn't have anything for that one. However, I was certain that this was information that Morgan would want to know about.

"Okay, then perhaps this should be brought to somebody in the Supernatural community." Now I was grasping at straws. "And when you say terrorism...what exactly are you talking about if I can ask?"

In books, movies, and television, when the hero or heroine embarks on some mission, journey or adventure, there is usually a scene where you, the audience, are privy to some secret piece of information. So, you go in to the story at least having an idea what was going on. Not here. You get to be as confused as I am. I had not heard about any recent act that could constitute terrorism.

"The home of the sidhe has been violated and many deaths have come as a result. Our woods have been razed...they came without warning with their evil machines. The cutting and burning..." and her voice broke.

Suddenly, this angry child was nothing more than a sad, frightened little girl, yet there was something odd in her eyes. Perhaps it was sadness, or maybe she was pissed. Since I knew nothing about faeries, I could not begin to guess. I do know that, if I had been of the warm-blooded sort, it might have mode my blood run just a bit cold. The others had moved closer and began to nestle up to Merriette. They were stroking her hair and caressing her skin. Some of it was dangerously close to inappropriate, but she seemed to welcome it.

"So this...?"

Again, I was forced to sort of wave my arms around to indicate the entire mall, and that is when I noticed; people were sort of frozen. Not in the ice cold version, but more of the confused and "what the hell am I doing here with Larry the Cable Guy sitting beside me with his pants down" sort of way. As I let my gaze sweep the area, I saw people with similar expressions, as if they woke from a strange dream to discover that their life had become a nightmare.

"This is a message," Merriette hissed. "This will get the attention of those pompous asses and force them to deal with the fey personally. And when they do...they will perish."

I was absolutely not getting it. There was a lot going on here and none of it was making the slightest bit of sense to me. I did not have one thing to grab on to and be able to hand over to Morgan other than a dead Faeire Godmother.

"Okay," I raised my hands in the gesture that I hoped indicated that I wanted her to slow down, "I need you to start from the beginning. First, tell me who came to your...sidhe? Was that the word? Did I say it right" This at least earned me a begrudging nod. "I am assuming that is your home. So who came to your home and destroyed it?"

I was feeling pretty good about my questions. I figured that this would make everything easier. This being an investigator or private detective for the Supernatural community could not be so hard.

Have you ever asked a question that seemed simple enough, but when you got the answer, it blasted a hole in your world? I'm not talking about questions like "Whose underwear are these?" You pretty much already know the answer, or at least you already know that they aren't yours, so you are at least somewhat ready in advance with the knowledge that the answer is going to be unpleasant.

What I am talking about are questions like, "So, Doc, are we all done here?" or "Mommy, what time is Daddy going to come home?" Then you get answers like, "Actually, we need to run some more tests..." or "The second Tuesday of Never!"

"The Templars!" Merriette only spoke two words, but they plunged an icy dagger into my heart.

That Ghoul Ava Kicks Some Faerie A**

3

Girls On Film

I was in my Corvette, the music was blasting and the self-proclaimed Prince of Darkness, His Royal Ozzness, was mocking my very thoughts as he strained with the high notes on the live version of *I Don't Know*. I had listened to everything that Merriette told me. But I had the feeling that there was something that did not add up.

In short, some upper level management type from the Templars was a fairly well known developer. For no reason that could be given by any of the faerie girls, a convoy of dozers and assorted construction and logging trucks rolled into the land that had been given to the fey in some agreement that went back several hundred years (according to the only side of the story that I had heard thus far).

To make matters worse, I guess they were accompanied by some sort of "goon squad" (my words, not Merriette's) that achieved the impossible: they entered the sidhe. From what I gather, no being is able to enter a fey stronghold without an escort from a faerie with a blood tie to the clan that resides there. Supposedly, the ground itself will not let anything pass without one of the locals acting as chaperon or opening the ways.

When this group of black clad invaders came, they did the next on a list of impossibilities: they began killing every faerie they encountered. Young, old, male, female…it was indiscriminate slaughter. However, they beelined for the chamber of the Faerie Godmother and, once there, they executed her entire entourage as well as the Godmother herself.

I may not be Cagney or Lacey, but this was sounding to me like an inside job. Somebody within the sidhe had sold them out. My only problem was that, even from what little I do understand about the politics in this Supernatural realm, the Templars would know better.

I did manage to convince the faeries to leave the mall. Of course the damage was already done. As I was getting in to my car, I saw news vans from every network pulling in to the mall parking lot. I did not dare to think how this would be spun by the talking heads.

Give them a gunman, a handful of innocent victims culminating in a suicide-by-cop conclusion, and they are all over it with catchy slogans, tag lines, and bright graphics accompanied by ominous music. This was the opposite of that. What they were walking in to was almost a public orgy.

People were in a daze and the confusion was visible on the faces of men and women alike. Although, to be honest, a lot of the men had trouble hiding smirks and grins…mostly. I passed one guy who was trying to delicately untangle himself from a lady that was easily in her late eighties. He was caught on her oxygen tube and, bless his heart, he was doing everything in his power not to pull that thing loose from her nostrils or the small tank that it was attached to at the other end which was fastened securely to her walker that lay a few feet away from her discarded Depends. Yeah, that guy wasn't smiling at all. But granny was glowing…which was only a little creepy.

By the time I hit the freeway, I had tried five times to call Lisa; each time I was dumped to voice mail after the first ring. That meant she either had her phone turned off, or she was hitting the "reject" button. A bad feeling was beginning to grow in my belly.

David Bowie was now encouraging everybody to put on their red shoes in a song that I hated until I discovered that it was the legendary Stevie Ray Vaughn playing guitar on the track of *Let's Dance*. Such a tragic waste of talent. Why can't airplanes with the Mileys and Brittanys and Lindsays crash into mountains? Why is it always the talented people...the Stevie Rays, Big Boppers, Buddy Hollys and Ritchie Valens?

As I pulled in to the driveway, something flashed across my field of vision. *No! Not now!* I screamed in my head.

In less time than it takes to snap your fingers, my hands and feet went on the defensive as my long, razor sharp talons sprouted where my recently painted nails had once been. Thankfully, I was already parked and quickly let go of my steering wheel as well as lifted my feet off the floorboard. A quick inspection revealed that I had not even put a crease in the leather wrap of my steering wheel or snagged the floor mat. When my door opened, I sprang.

"Ava! It's me!" a voice said from above me.

Yep, I had leapt from my car with the intention of rending whatever was out there into meat confetti. Only, vampires have that damn hyperspace-jump gear when it comes to speed. My target had managed to not only avoid me, but make it safely to a branch about twenty feet above my head.

"What the hell were you thinking, Jeremy?" I growled.

"I wanted to surprise you." He sounded funny...like his feelings were hurt. "I take it you are not having a good night?"

His words were rattling around in my head, but I was stuck on something else at the moment. While my switchblade finger and toenails are nothing new to me—I have the open account at the Nike Store to prove it since any shoes I wear at the time are instantly ruined—this sudden burst of anger is very much not like me.

Seriously, I was ready to gut whoever or whatever had been outside my car. There was not even a thought about maybe checking it out. My first reaction had been to kill.

Hmm. Peculiar.

"...and when Belinda called me and said that I needed to get right over to your place and check on you—" Jeremy had been talking while I was in Ava Land. I probably would have continued to ignore him if he had not mentioned the queen of bitchy vampires, Belinda Yates.

"Wait!" I held up a hand to shut Jeremy up. "Why would Belinda send anybody to check on me?"

The look of irritation on Jeremy's face was brief. I think he was getting used to the idea that I tend to mentally wander when people talk.

"The news? There was some sort of massive protest over at the Eastport Mall. The cameras were not allowed in, but they said it was like those things where a bunch of people show up and do one of those choreographed dances...only this was...sex?" He sounded confused and like he was not really believing the words coming out of his mouth.

"Okay, so what does that have to do with me? Why would Belinda send one of her vampires to check on me?"

"So you don't know..."

Could a vampire become more pale? It sure seemed like Jeremy did at that moment.

"Don't know what?" I had a feeling that I knew more than he or Belinda.

"Your human—err...Lisa?" He had the sense to look embarrassed (well, as much as a vampire can anyway). He knew that I hated it when any of my fellow Supes referred to Lisa as "my" human. She was a human, yes. But she was not *my* anything.

"What about her?" Now he had my undivided attention.

"It was only in the background, and it is unlikely that anybody even paid it any attention, but Belinda spotted it instantly when—"

"Just spit it out!" I snapped. I could tell that he was not very happy about whatever it was that he had been sent to tell me.

"A dark van with no windows pulled up to the curb as Lisa was walking by, and whoever was inside reached out, snatched her, yanked her inside and took off."

For some reason, there was a peculiar buzzing noise in my

head. I stood there staring at Jeremy the vampire (and my some-times love interest despite the fact that we can't kiss...eww!) with the knowledge that I should feel something. I knew that I should be scared for Lisa, that I should be terribly upset. On-ly...I felt...

Nothing.

For the first time, I actually felt completely dead. There was no emotion. No anger, no fear. Just that strange buzzing like a hive of huge bumblebees was trapped in my head.

Only, there was this sort of "awareness" that seemed to be oozing in through all of the cracks. I could sense my fingers and toes. With no more thought than you would give a wink, I re-tracted my fingernails and then my toenails. Just as easily, I extended them again.

Next, I activated (I imagine there might be a better word, but this is the best I can come up with for now...maybe the cal-endar will help) Sharkmouth. In a flash, my mouth morphed and the three rows of needle-like teeth dropped.

The buzzing subsided to a hum and I continued to whip through all of my little weapons like somebody who just discov-ered a remote control. I have no idea what it must have looked like to Jeremy. I do know that he had retreated up a few more branches in the tree by the time I returned my attention his way.

"That's new," was all he managed to say.

"I know, right?"

Focus, Ava...Lisa is in trouble.

I headed for the front door, motioning for Jeremy to follow me inside. I had just realized that I went through my ghoulish arsenal while standing in my driveway. I was one Alice Kravitz away from being discovered.

I did not look to see if Jeremy the vampire followed or not, I just assumed that he would. As soon as I turned the knob and opened the door, I knew there was trouble. I could smell it...literally.

Okay, so just a quick note. I have never been confused with the smart kids. I was a straight 'C' student in high school and was on the fast track to becoming a living model of the character

'Flo' from that old 70s sitcom, *Alice*. If your brain did not immediately blurt, "Kiss my grits!" then I pity you. Anyways, I have an actual pet peeve when it comes to a certain grammatical error that is simply out of control in today's younger folks. Can people stop using the word 'literally' until they look it up in the dictionary and understand its actual meaning. For instance, you will not 'literally scream your head off' or 'literally die of embarrassment'.

Anyways, back to me entering the house and smelling something. This was not good. Something had decided to break in and was waiting just beyond the entry hall. I could hear the short, shallow breaths of somebody who was getting very worked up.

"You have five seconds to step out and identify yourself...or I won't be responsible for what happens next."

Snick. (Eat your heart out Wolverine!)

With the slightest thought, fingers and toes went switchblade. Oh! How cool! It still works. I have no idea what has triggered this new change, but I am digging it the most right now.

"Five."

I heard the person gasp, and then hold his or her breath like that would suddenly help. Perhaps if their heart was not beating at the inside of the chest like Tommy Lee in his Tilt-A-Whirl drum kit...

"Four."

Something made a metallic scraping sound, like a blade being drawn.

"Three."

A sharp exhale.

"Twoone."

I cheated. I may have blurted those last two numbers a bit quick as I sprang to the bannister of my wraparound staircase and spun so that I was now looking down on my intruder. Obviously the person had not seen or heard me vault past, but the scrape of my nails on the solid oak bannister caused him—it was definitely a him—to spin in my direction. My perfect vision,

26

which allowed me to see in the dark, registered the look of surprise in cueball's face.

"What the—" was all he managed before Jeremy pounced and knocked this goon flat on his back.

It was actually a bit comical. Seriously, Jeremy does not look all that tough. He is slender and average when it comes to size, and this intruder was big enough to go head-to-head with the Hulkster. (I'm talking about the one who wears red and yellow, tells kids to say their prayers and eat their vitamins…and then sells his soul to reality television where he became little more than a glorified pimp for his creepy daughter…not the big green one. Just wanted to be clear.)

"You made a very big mistake," Jeremy hissed, his fangs snapping very close to the tip of the stranger's nose.

"I-I-I—" the man was stuttering like Porky Pig.

"You have made a terrible mistake," Jeremy repeated, and his voice was taking on some sort of odd quality. It sounded almost like he was singing a lullaby.

"I have made a terrible mistake," the man slurred. He sounded drunk.

"You should not be here," Jeremy continued.

I hopped off my bannister and hurried down to where he was sitting on the man's chest. The man was staring straight up and into Jeremy's eyes. Now I got it; he was using that vampire hypnosis thing. And that made me blurt out, "Tell him, 'These are not the droids you are looking for.'"

Jeremy sighed. I think I saw his shoulders slump just a little. "These are not the droids you are looking for."

"These are not the droids I am looking for."

Yay!

He shot a glance at me. His fangs were out and he caught just enough of the entryway light for them to glint. "Are you done playing?"

I nodded.

"Who sent you?" Jeremy returned his attention to L'il Hulkster.

Nothing. The man simply stared up at Jeremy with a blank

expression. Jeremy repeated his question twice more. Blood began to trickle from the man's nose. I saw Jeremy give an involuntary shudder. I imagine that would be like waving a candy bar at me during my worst PMS. You might not get all of your hand back. Well, at least that used to be the case. I didn't have any of those problems now that I was a ghoul. Who said being dead doesn't have its advantages.

"Something is wrong here," Jeremy whispered.

"Why is his nose—" I didn't get to finish that sentence.

A wave of something sweet filled my nostrils just as the man's eyes ruptured and blood began to pour from every hole in his head. Yep, eyes, ears, nose and mouth…all gushing. It was too much for Jeremy and he reared back and struck, teeth sinking into the man's throat.

Sharkmouth came unbidden, and I almost shoved Jeremy aside…except he suddenly shot backwards like he had been launched from a catapult. He went right out the front door. Meanwhile, the blood fountain that had once been a man started to convulse. Great, I was going to have some serious scrubbing to do. He was making my wall look like a Jackson Pollack painting. (Bet you weren't expecting me to pull something like that out of the air. Yeah, well don't be too impressed. I saw the movie during a period of my life where I had a huge crush on Ed Harris.)

"Ava?" a voice called from the doorway.

"Kinda busy!" I yelled over my shoulder as the man stood.

By now, he had blood leaking from his pores. His face was a mask of red, and I was having a very difficult time not just chowing down on him. My only problem was that he was still alive. Ghouls only eat the dead. Oh well, in for a penny…in for a pound.

My grandmother used to say that all the time when she was playing BINGO down at the church. I didn't really know what she was talking about, but she would shift from one or two cards in front of her to having like ten or more. I would sit there drinking my Grape Nehi that she would buy from the old machine by the front door and watch her go crazy with her little ink blot bottle thingy.

Hmm…bloody L'il Hulkster had managed to close half the distance between us. I better do something. My claws did not simply slice his throat as I had intended; his head landed beside his feet with a heavy thud. The body took another couple of steps before it figured out the problem and finally collapsed.

Like that talking plant said in *Little Shop of Horrors*…

SUPPER TIME!

I tore into that body like Augustus Gloop did to the chocolate river in *Willy Wonka*. It took me a few minutes, and not once did my thoughts ever turn to the fate of my vampire pal. Hmm…maybe we weren't all that close. I mean, if I was more intent on eating than I was checking on whether or not Jeremy had been impaled on a tree branch when he was hurled out my front door, then maybe it *was* just about the sex.

Just as I finished and was dabbing at the corners of my mouth with a moist towelette, Jeremy came through my front door. Something on my ghoul radar pinged. He did not need to be invited in. That was curious. Belinda had been over on more than one occasion, but I had to invite her in every single time.

"I'm okay…thanks for asking."

Great, vamp with an attitude. Not exactly what I needed at the moment.

"Yeah, yeah…hope you're all better," I waved a dismissive hand at him. "Now tell me what the heck is going on with Lisa. What did Belinda see and why does she care?"

There was an uncomfortable moment of silence, and then he spoke. "Belinda and Lisa have been meeting the past few weeks. Not every night, but periodically. And before you ask, I have no idea what they were meeting about. Anyway, when Belinda saw what she did, she told me to get over here right away and see if you were…"

"Dead?" I asked.

I felt something inside me tingle just a bit. Tonight was certainly becoming a night of new experiences. I imagine that I could ask Morgan, but I had a feeling that she would only tell me what she wanted me to know. No, I would be taking my questions elsewhere. That would at least give me a better shot at getting a complete answer. Also, it would keep Morgan from knowing all my new tricks.

"...and that dagger he had was actual cold steel. So I think it is safe to say that whoever sent him, knows what you are and how to kill you."

"Wait!" I held my hand up. Jeremy had just said something that was important. "How do you know that this dagger is cold steel?"

"It's stamped on the sheath for one." Jeremy pointed.

I turned and looked. Now I was confused. It must have shown.

"You didn't know that Cold Steel is a company?" (See, this is a case of not hearing capital letters when people talk. This entire time, I thought that Cold Steel was some special process. *Now* I learn it is a company.)

"Nope." I figured that this was one of those times to say very little in hopes that I would be given some actual information.

"Cold Steel is a company that is owned by the Templars. During the period where they were at war with the Supernatural community, they made it a practice to try and take some of them alive." He looked at me with the vampire equivalent of a question on his face. "Has nobody taught you any of this? Seriously, this is some of the first stuff that you are indoctrinated on when you become part of the community."

Great...more reasons to not trust Morgan. Those were starting to pile up. I had a feeling that she and I were on a collision course for a very nasty scene.

"Anyway, over the years...decades really...they began to discover various things that would do harm to some of us. As they learned, they began to create weapons designed for the specific practice of killing vampire, werewolves, trolls—"

"Ghouls," I added, waving my hands for him to just get on with it.

"Oh...yeah. So they have been making weapons for centuries. There have been different names, but for the last thirty or so

30

years they have been under the Cold Steel label. But they are very cautious about who has access to their special product line. If they are sending thugs and hit men, this might mean that another war is about to happen."

Hmm. This was becoming so much more than I had signed on for. I mean, my job had been to get the faeries in the mall to stop turning people into perverted little horn dogs. Nothing was said about wars or any of that stuff. And honestly, that all sounded like a bit much for me.

"...learn to do that?"

"Huh?" I had heard enough to guess what he was talking about. "Oh...this?" I made my switchfingers and toes extend and then retract.

"Uhh...yeah. How long have you been able to do that?"

None of his business. I simply smiled. At least I think so, it is sort of hard to tell when you are rocking the Sharkmouth. One thing was for sure...if I could control this, I could finally buy those Jimmy Choos that I saw downtown.

That Ghoul Ava Kicks Some Faerie A**

4

Slip of the Tongue

"I am sick and tired of you not telling me things and then I end up in the middle of a vampire power struggle...attempted faerie genocide...a war against the entire supernatural community!"

I had been yelling for quite a while, and Morgan was still just standing there with absolutely no expression on her face. Well, maybe it was time to see if she actually could change the look on her face, or if it was frozen in that Nicole Kidman Botox expression that she wore all the time.

Snick.

My fingers only, since I was wearing these really nice purple Nikes and did not want to ruin them just yet. I waved my hands in a display that would have made David Copperfield proud. I may have even said, "Ta-da!"

Nothing from the glacier that is Morgan.

"Seriously?" I exploded. "You just saw me bring on the claws at will and you don't even blink?"

"You are a ghoul, Ava," Morgan said with no inflection. "Just as a child learns to walk and eventually run, you will learn to control your...abilities."

33

"Yeah, but don't parents usually get excited when their kids take the first step?"

"I am not your parent."

I had something on the tip of my tongue, but it dissolved like that sour stuff inside a Zotz pop. She was absolutely correct. She was not my mom or dad. She was my employer (for lack of a better term).

"Okay…" I had to change tactics. "But does this not make me somewhat more useful to you?"

"Undoubtedly. But I was under the assumption that you called me here because of the situation with the faeries. Do you know how many phone calls I have had to make to get that stuff pulled from the news?"

She could do that? Wow. Taking a juicy story like that from the media was probably more difficult than prying a Black Friday special from a Walmart shopper's hands.

And I know I have said this before, but can somebody tell me why we still rant and rave on the social media about stores being open on Thanksgiving night? Seriously, if you are able to overcome your food coma and want to give the economy a boost by spending your money on ten-for-a-dollar socks or underwear…BIG DEAL! Don't like it? Stay home. People seem to just look for excuses to be indignant these days.

"Speaking of the news, now that I have told you what the faeries revealed, when do I get paid?"

I wasn't exactly hurting for money…yet. But why wait until the cupboards were bare? Plus, now that I was in control of my switchblade claws, Mama wants to go shoppin'!

"As soon as the job is finished," Morgan said coolly.

It took me a moment, but I eventually figured out that she meant there was still more to this job. I sure did not know what the heck she could be talking about. I had busted up the little faerie freak-fest. I'd even discovered some stuff that went beyond what I considered to be my assigned task.

"Have you spoken to the Godmother?" Morgan asked.

"No, you never said—"

"Seriously, do I have to explain every single detail to you?"

34

Apparently. Sure, I only thought that word, but I guess Morgan saw it on my face.

"The only person that can allow or properly punish such an act as the one that those faeries committed is the Godmother."

"Did you miss the part about the Godmother being killed?"

"The faeries have another. They would not go the day without appointing a new Godmother. That is their way."

Hmm. Well they never mentioned anything of that sort to me. Fine, I guess I could go seek them out and talk to whoever this new Godmother might be.

"As for Lisa, I have resources looking for her right now." Morgan was apparently done with the faeries business. "Naturally, the van had no plates and was about as unremarkable as possible, but we have a few leads and should know something soon."

That was interesting. She actually sounded...concerned. First, for Morgan to have any real emotion in her voice was already a pretty big deal, but for her to sound this concerned about a "mere human" (her words, never mine) was definitely worth noting.

"Anything that I can do?" It seemed like a logical question.

"You need to stay on task. Let me take care of this, Ava."

That was weird. She was sounding all nice and stuff. I didn't trust it one bit. In fact, I was now certain that there was way more going on than I was being let in on when it came to my friend, Lisa Jenkins. First Belinda, and now Morgan.

"I want you to get this faerie issue handled right away," Morgan was back to talking about the job. All that concern may well have never existed...or perhaps it was just a figment of my imagination.

"Aye-aye, boss." I snapped to attention and saluted. Before I even finished...she was gone. I hated when she did that.

I went to my basement and pulled a fresh corpse from the walk-in refrigerator and had a quick meal. Don't judge me...I get hungry too.

"So...trouble brewing?" a voice cooed from behind a steel door.

"Can it, Adrianna." I was in no mood for her nonsense today.

Adrianna, former self-proclaimed Queen of the Zombies, and current occupant of an extra-dimensional jail cell in my basement pressed her face up against the small slit so that I could see her eyes. I did not need to see her mouth to know that she was smiling.

Betty, a very powerful Supernatural that has not really told me as much about herself as she has about Morgan and the history of ghouls, created the cell. (I don't know how, so don't ask.) She intends to keep Adrianna here until a "more permanent solution" is ready to be implemented. I have no idea who—or more likely, *what*—will be taking on that job, but I hope they finish soon.

"Maybe I can help." Adrianna's voice changed just a bit. I heard…no…that can't be right.

"Are you trying to pretend that you actually care?" I tried not to laugh, but seriously…you read that last little adventure, so I don't need to tell you just how out of character her caring about anything besides herself would be.

"It involves the human, Lisa. So…yes, I do actually care."

What in the heck was it about Lisa lately? It seemed that every single Supernatural that I ran into was suddenly taken by Lisa. Morgan, Belinda, Jeremy…and now Adrianna?

"Why would you care about a human?" I snapped as I slipped in to Sharkmouth mode and made short work of some little old lady who had passed away in her apartment unbeknownst to her neighbors.

Wait…did I just use the word "unbeknownst" in a sentence? Yay me!

"…become the eventual leader of the Templar order, then it might do me some good not to be on her bad side. Not that I think Betty is going to let me live long enough to actually see that happen."

Huh? Who was going to become the leader of the Templars? Was she talking about Lisa? Was I missing a memo?

"Wait!" Adrianna hissed. "You didn't know! How is that

Slip of the Tongue

possible? The meetings in your own home. Surely with your abilities they could not be able to meet here and you not overhear every single word that was being said…"

Adrianna continued to talk, but I had switched her off. I ran the last several weeks through my head. I did not recall so much as one single meeting that had taken place. However, a few things did suddenly stand out.

Over the weeks, there had been times when Betty had been here. It was during those times that she would usually spell Arianna into what was basically a coma so that the cell could be cleaned out. Lisa had always offered to help. I was making some big leaps here. It would be nice if I got some confirmation.

I ran upstairs and logged onto my computer. With a few keystrokes, I made a check of the video log history. Sure enough, there were a few entries that had been deleted. Usually no more than ten or fifteen minutes. But when I checked, they were a day or so after one of Betty's visits.

Now, I am not ever going to be confused with one of those television detectives, but maybe all this stuff that I was doing was paying off. I had a hunch, and if I was correct…

I was scared.

If my guess was right, then it could damage, if not outright end, Lisa's and my relationship forever. I had to make a decision. Did I want the answer?

A few minutes later, I was standing outside of Adrianna's cell door again. I had to know.

"So, you don't recall having any recent injuries?" I asked.

"For the hundredth time, Ava, I don't get injuries," Adrianna huffed.

"Right, you have some sort of regenerative ability…like a salamander."

"I beg your pardon!"

"Sure…you cut off a salamander's tail and it will eventually grow back. Basically, you are saying that you do the same thing."

"You have a real knack for trivializing that which you don't understand."

"No, what I do have is a knack for is taking something that most folks would complicate with a bunch of gobbledy gook and making sense out of it."

"And so you just want me to let you cut a piece of me off for you to simply snack on?"

Adrianna returned to my request. I admit, when she said it like that…it did sound kind of icky.

"I already said that in exchange, I will request that Betty not eventually have you executed."

Actually, that was a pretty easy offer to make. I already knew that the old woman was not planning an execution. Nope, she had something else in mind, and I was only able to understand part of it—the part that had to do with me, imagine that—but I was almost certain that, once Adrianna discovered the actual plan, she would probably prefer death.

"I don't want you to request anything…I want your word that it will not happen. I want you to agree to a binding."

"So I get a few slivers of skin and you want me to submit to some magical thing that I imagine has nasty consequences if I don't live up to my end."

"That just about sums it up," Adrianna snapped. I saw her eyes move and knew that she had nodded her head.

Since I was already aware, at least to some extent, what Betty had in mind, not to mention the fact that I had fired off about a million questions when I was let in on the secret, I decided that I was not in any real danger. Betty's plan just sounded too out there for me to believe.

"Fine," I agreed.

Adrianna then told me all the stuff that I needed to do for this binding ritual. Mostly it involved cutting my palm and mixing the drops in a copper bowl and then cooking it off while chanting some funky words that I am pretty sure were Latin.

Once I was done, I waited. Nothing happened. No breeze or distant wails of tormented souls in the underworld. No flicker of lights or strange bodily sensations. I almost asked if she was sure that we had done it right, then I remembered something: I DIDN'T CARE! After all, this was Adrianna. Seriously, you read the last book, so you have to know why I really did not care if I was getting one over on her.

"Okay, hand me a knife," Adrianna said from the other side of the door.

All of a sudden, I saw a big flaw in my plan. I had seen enough movies set in jails and prisons to know that you never gave the inmates sharp stabby things. Oh well, it couldn't be helped.

"Do you need something special?"

"Something special?" Adrianna sounded perplexed.

"Like a special sort of knife or ornate dagger?"

"You really do need to stop watching all those ridiculous movies," Adrianna said with what sounded like a pleasant laugh. I was not about to be fooled, but seriously, it was like we were sharing a moment.

I waited patiently. Even without my super sensitive hearing, I was able to hear her make a hissing sound like she sucked in a breath really hard. I guess she feels pain just like anybody—or anything, for that matter—else.

She handed me the knife as well as a piece of flesh that had me drooling like crazy. I was actually surprised that I was able to hold off for a few seconds and put the knife away before switching to Sharkmouth. And then...

"Well, nothing seemed to happen," I sighed.

"Check the tape, Ava," a voice said from beyond the cell door.

I didn't know why. That was a clue.

I went to the computer and brought up the file for the past twenty minutes of footage taken from my basement camera. I did not need the audio; I just let the picture roll. Hmm...there I was sitting on the floor. Adrianna's cell door was wide open! Hmm...why wasn't she coming out? I could see her Royal Zombieness just standing there. She was talking and I was nodding. Maybe I did need the audio.

"...makes perfect sense that she would put some sort of hex on the entry way to keep me in if I should somehow manage to get the door open," Adrianna was complaining.

"I'm sorry...well, not actually sorry, but...heck, I don't know what I'm feeling." I sounded drunk. The last time I'd been drunk was after eating this little old man who happened to be a zombie...and Betty's husband...but why am I telling you? You already read the book.

"I suggest that you figure out why your friend has felt the need to keep these secrets from you," Adrianna said. Her left hand came up and she very tentatively reached forward. I saw a flash of blue sparks and she quickly yanked her hand back, a look of annoyance clear on her face.

Hmm. I should have known that she was up to something. There was really no other reason for her to make any deals with me. That was strange, I could recall all of that part of our conversation, but everything that was playing out on the video might as well have happened to somebody else.

"Maybe I should have let Belinda take a nip that night," I whined. Great, now I was sounding like the weepy drunk. All that I needed to hear next was—

"I really do love you, Adrianna. We just got off on the wrong foot, but I think we can still be friends."

And there it was; absolute proof that I was drunk out of my head. But how?

"So every time that little human was coming in here, she was taking a slice of me, then, somehow she was slipping it to you so that you would be out of it for a while. And that was when she was having the Templars meet here," Adrianna explained.

"You keep saying that," I slurred. I watched as I leaned against the wall and slid over to lay on the floor beside the open cell door.

"That is because I want to make sure that you see and hear this when you roll that video back. Something is going on, and if you are, as you say, the only key to my continued existence, then I obviously need you to stay alive."

Interesting. What had I spilled to her while I was all loopy? I could play it back later and find out. Right now, I had more important worries. I stopped the playback and returned to the basement.

"So, why would she do that? Why would she drug me and then have her meetings here, or whatever was going on? I mean, why not just meet someplace else?" I asked. It was not really a question that I expected her to have an answer for, but I still wanted to get it out there just in case she had anything to offer.

"Unfortunately, I am not graced with your ability to hear so acutely, otherwise, I would have something to offer, However, I do know that you were always present upstairs while these meetings took place. That is why I assumed that whatever was going on was some plot of yours."

Now I was stumped and annoyed. Lisa was the one person, Supernatural or otherwise, that I believed I could trust. Turns out that I was probably wrong about that one.

It was almost as bad as my history with men.

That Ghoul Ava Kicks Some Faerie A**

5

Screaming in the Night

I think the best thing about being a creature of the night is the fact that traffic is almost non-existent. I had my Corvette on Highway 26, headed towards the town of Tillamook. The speedometer was a testament to how I was in complete agreement with Sammy Hagar. I can't drive fifty-five either. In fact, the white lines looked like a solid stripe they were whizzing by so fast.

After mulling things over, I decided that I would have to go meet with the faeries. Merriette was not all that enthusiastic, but she agreed to meet me as long as I agreed to do so at the place of her choosing. I had no idea why she chose Tillamook, but I figured it would be a nice chance to get out on the road and clear my head.

"Miss," the voice said in barley a whisper from my passenger's seat, "is it absolutely necessary for you to drive this fast?"

Aoife the siren had arrived at my house just as I was about to leave. She said that she had heard the terrible news about Lisa and wanted to be sure that I was okay. I guess she saw through my attempted lie, because she gave me this big hug that lasted so long that it almost became uncomfortable.

You know, for somebody who is so steadfast in her claims of being straight…I have some real issues with being turned on by super-hot females. However, in my defense, a woman's body is far more pleasing to look at than a man's. Seriously, you don't have to be even a teensy bit gay to be on board with that realization. I just wish some of the men out there would get the memo. Fellas, your 'junk' is not at all sexy. Useful? Certainly. Sexy? Not even a little bit. You can't bend or squat without looking ridiculous.

That stuff just dangling? I'm surprised more women aren't gay. I could go on for pages about how unappealing that little bag is that houses your berries. However, used properly, you are sufficient…just not as sexy as you might think.

KISS was singing, more specifically, Paul Stanley. He was telling me that he would love me (or somebody anyways) "Forever". However, Aoife was also talking, and her voice was becoming more frantic. That was when I realized that I was hitting the winding curves of the Coastal Range. The uphill slope was getting steeper and the curves were becoming windier…more windy? Twisty? You get the idea.

I was loving the way that my Corvette hugged the curves. It was like the best roller coaster in the world made even better because I was steering it. Apparently Aoife did not share my joy. She was gripping the dashboard with both hands, and I was pretty sure that she was going to leave her finger impressions on it if she held on much longer. I sighed and slowed down.

"So, you say that you have been to see these faeries before?" I decided that a little conversation might take her mind off of my driving. I had backed it all the way down to around eighty and she was still not looking very relaxed.

"A few times," Aoife said in her beautiful and melodic voice. "The Godmother…*Ar dheis Dé go raibh a h-anam.* (which sounded like 'ahr yesh day go rav hu ha-num' and she later told me that was basically the Gaelic equivalent of saying "Rest in peace") She always enjoyed having some of us sirens over for different festivals. How she loved to hear us sing."

"But you say that they have never lived on this side of the

44

Oregon Coastal Range because of an agreement with…goblins?"

Yeah, I was hearing the words that were coming out of my mouth, I just was having a real hard time believing them. I guess the first few years as a Supernatural come with a pretty steep learning curve. Goblins, vampires, sirens, faeries, trolls. All of it was starting to pile up. I was quickly becoming very aware of how much I did not know.

"The goblins swore that they would leave the faeries in peace as long as the border was respected," Aoife explained much like you might tell somebody that you liked peanut butter and jelly. In other words, this was absolutely nothing to her except a fact. "If they have come over here as you say, then this cannot bode well. They would be offering themselves freely to the goblins as chattel. They would become servants not only of the typical sort, but also as breeder stock. Goblins love keeping faeries as sex slaves. They are very aware of their own repulsive nature and find pleasure in being able to rut and paw at something so beautiful."

"Wait, I'm not putting you in any harm by bringing you here, am I?" That was the last thing I needed at the moment.

"Certainly not," Aoife laughed. "No goblin would dare touch a siren. For one, we could bespell one of those weak-minded simpletons even easier than a standard human mortal, and for another…no…that is pretty much it. They are weak-minded simpletons and would not make it past the first few seconds of the simplest bewitching song sung by one of our youngest children able to weave the words."

It sounded like a lot of smack talk if you asked me, but I would just take her at her word. However, now I was starting to get curious about what a goblin might look like. I mean, I had never seen one unless you counted the movie *The Hobbit*, and I was almost certain that they would not look anything like those creatures from the movies.

As we cruised into town, I started to see these peculiar markings painted on the various street signs. They were amazingly identical, so whoever the tagger was, he or she had a very precise hand.

I reached the main strip of downtown Tillamook and turned in to the mall that Merriette had told me to meet her at. Thankfully I was parked when I noticed that whoever the mystery tagger was had created a ten foot high version of whatever funky symbol I had been seeing as I rolled in to town, otherwise I might have dinged my car.

"How the heck do they do it?" I whispered.

"What?" Aoife seemed oblivious as I stared in open-mouthed amazement at the glittering piece of graffiti that practically obscured the entire mall entry sign.

"Please tell me you can see that." I pointed out the source of my amazement.

"Oh that," she said with an almost dismissive wave of her hand. "For one, goblins can't actually be seen by the naked human eye. Many believe that it is because they are so hideous, that Mother Nature eventually had to tweak the makeup of the human eye to keep them safe. And they have always been known for their artistry. You don't think Michelangelo did that entire ceiling by himself do you. Silly humans…always thinking that they are far more capable than they really are."

Aoife began to laugh…and then it ended in a strangled cough. She actually looked afraid.

"Please, miss. I meant no disrespect."

"I'm not a human anymore, Aoife," I patted the siren on the knee. "Now, back to this goblin art. Does it say something, or is it just some sort of decoration?"

"It is a mark that makes it clear that this is their territory. Any who enter must declare themselves to the goblins or be seen as invaders."

"And that means what, exactly?"

"They are fair game. Goblins are not picky eaters," Aoife said way too casually.

"But I thought there were all these rules preventing Supernaturals from just taking each other out."

"There are, but before the accords were arranged and signed, the goblins never posted any sort of notice. They would just attack at will."

"And now they—" I started, but was interrupted by a sharp rap on my window. I looked but did not see anything.

"We need to get out of the car, miss," Aoife said in a very soft but firm voice.

"Why?" And then the smell hit me.

How do I describe this in a way that most people will relate? Okay...here goes nothing. Imagine a cow pasture or the livestock exhibit at the fair. Now, heat that up and add in an undertone of spoiled vinegar. You getting that? Can you feel a tanginess developing in the back of your throat? That is pretty much how goblins smell.

I still did not see anything, but when I opened my door, I had to give an extra push. Something was blocking my exit. It turned out to be about forty of the nasty little flea bags. And yes, goblins have fleas, I was not just being snarky. In fact, it seemed as if there were always one or two of them pausing to scratch much like a dog.

So, how to describe a goblin. Well, for one, they are only about two or three feet tall. Their bodies are a patchwork of hideous scars on their leathery patches of skin (a badge of honor for them, or so I am told) mixed with coarse tufts of fur. Their faces resemble a dog, and I was told that Pit Bulls are actually descendants from goblins. They have jutting lower jaws and long canine teeth that poke up and out at odd angles. Their ears are similar to pig ears and they have dark beady eyes. Oh...and they only have three fingers and a hooked claw that might be a thumb.

"You are in the land of the Cow Fart clan," a voice that sounded like the devil on helium spoke.

I kept a very straight face. It was not easy. Did I forget to mention that goblins prefer running around naked? Oh...and yes, the clan name was funny too. But I should probably share a few more tidbits about goblins. The males? Well, let's just say that they are lucky that they do not trip more often. Seriously, they would make some of the human male porn stars envious. And the women, much like dogs, they have four sets of breasts. And not the perky kind like Aoife or that you find in a magazine like

Playboy. Nope, these are the *National Geographic*-saggy types that swing back and forth in sync with their waddling owner. Oh yeah, goblins waddle.

"I am here to meet with Merriette. She told me to come here?" I said as I stepped out of my car.

I was going to say more, like introduce myself or something, when one of those nasty little freaks climbed up on the hood of my beautiful Corvette. I may have said something like "Shoo!" or words to that effect, but it was my backhand that sent the little vermin sprawling which caused the real uproar.

All of a sudden, I am looking at the points of around fifty or so little blades. Some were jagged and rusty looking, others pointy and clean, but the bottom line was that there were a lot of them, and they were all pointed at me.

"I wouldn't do that," Aoife said as she emerged from the passenger side.

The goblins did not seem to be taking her warning very seriously...until she made her next statement.

"Do you really want to tangle with a ghoul?"

Crickets. Seriously, I could hear crickets chirping. The entire parking lot was suddenly empty. I don't know how, but every single one of those little goblins had beat feet so fast that the Road Runner would have done a double-take.

I was about to ask Aoife what all that was about when I heard a shriek from nearby. Without hardly a thought, I kicked off my shoes and let all my claws extend. I loped off in the direction of that scream and quickly picked up a scent that was almost sickening in its sweetness. It was like the smell of cotton candy magnified by a million. (Notice how I didn't say "literally"?)

I reached the far side of the lot that was actually close to some sort of big pond. Standing at the water's edge were three goblins; they had a prisoner.

"Let go of the faerie," I growled.

It wasn't Merriette, but I was sure that I recognized this faerie from someplace. While that group at the mall were all younger and looked much like your average teenager, this one was older...like my age.

"We have been sent to convey a message," one of the goblins snorted. Yeah, goblins snort...it is almost like they are trying to inhale snot and speak at the same time. So basically...gross.

"I don't need any messages—" I started, but the little freak cut me off.

"You are in the land of the—"

"Cow Fart clan, yeah, I already got that message. Now let go of the faerie before I lose my temper." Two could play at the interrupting game.

"You are not here at our pleasure, ghoul."

"I'm not here at anybody's pleasure," I snapped. Although not entirely sure, I think he was just pretty much saying that I was trespassing. Whoop-de-freakin'-do!

"You are speaking to the ghoul, Ava Birch," Aoife stepped forward and fixed the trio with a pretty nasty glare. "The vanquisher of The Queen of the Zombies."

I am pretty sure that Adrianna would be tickled to know that her name still merited the use of capital letters. Of course I did have bigger problems at the moment than worrying about whether or not the resident of the magic cell in my basement was happy.

"We care nothing for that," one of the goblins snarled. He took a step forward and his willy swung back and forth like one of those pendulum thingies in a grandfather clock.

I was about to make a pretty lewd comment when the faerie spoke up. She had been looking at me funny this whole time, but it wasn't until she spoke that I realized why.

"She is friend of the vampire," she blurted.

That was when I recognized her. She had been at that pizza place the night of that fight between Jeremy and some of the locals. She and a group of faeries had been present...and a little tipsy if my memory served me correct.

For whatever reason, that made the goblins pause. They began to whisper amongst themselves. Fortunately for me, I have ghoulish hearing and was able to listen in.

49

"If she is friends to Belinda, this could go very bad for us," the first said.

"But the king has been under her thumb for over a century, perhaps it is time that we let him die and proceed with the challenge for the throne," Dangling Willy spoke.

He looked over his shoulder at me and realized that I could hear. However, instead of telling the others to be quiet, he simply grabbed his junk and waved it at me. Yep, he had enough to grip in his fist and still shake what was left at me like a soggy, limp sausage before returning his attention to the others.

"And if she is not lying about the faeries calling for her, we would be seen as taking an aggressive action against an ambassador," the third, and up until this point, silent, member of the group added.

"We are goblins, we do not answer to some ghoul, nor do we care any longer about the pact with the faeries…Fraylee has made that all a moot point."

"But Fraylee also told us not to bring attention before he was ready lest the plan be ruined," the first insisted.

"What do we care about what Fraylee wants," Dangling Willy snapped. He glanced at me again, but this time, I swear he winked at me.

I decided that was either more of him just being cocky (see what I did there?) or he was trying to signal me about something. I took a few steps in their direction and brought my hands up in a bit of a Freddy Krueger pose where I let my fingers wave enough so that my razor claws caught just a glint of moonlight.

"Stand fast, ghoul!" a voice called from behind me.

Damn, I thought, *how had that happened?* I turned to discover a short, middle-aged looking, partially balding man with a waistline that screamed the impossibility that he should be able to creep up on anybody…much less me. My hearing should prevent me from being snuck up on by just about anything. In fact, the only thing that I had encountered so far with the ability to—

"My name is Blue," the man said with a hint of a smile.

"Like the color?" I asked, turning just enough so that I had the goblins to my right and this weirdo to my left.

"Actually, it is short for Blumegastrickfiggernilly."

"Oh…so just Blue then, I getcha."

"I am the Psychic for this region. My area stretches from Astoria, all the way down to Newport. You are not one of my people, so perhaps you can explain why you are here in my territory?"

I did seem to recall Morgan saying something about how Psychics were very territorial and that there was some degree of protocol when it came to travel.

"I heard rumor that a ghoul had been spotted in the Portland area, but when Morgan made no announcement that she had claimed one, most of us dismissed it as fanciful talk. Yet…here you are standing before my very eyes. Are you, in fact, from Portland?" Blue stepped closer. He was studying me in a way that made me feel a bit uncomfortable.

"Maybe." I decided that I was not just going to give up information for free. If this creep wanted to know something, he was going to have to give to receive.

"You show no indications of being claimed," he muttered. Actually, now he seemed more involved with himself than with me. He had his lips pursed and his chin in his hand as he cocked his head one way and then another. "If you were in Morgan's region and she has let you slip past…"

Suddenly he seemed to remember that I was actually standing there. He shook himself and stood up straight. With a wave of his hand, he shooed the goblins away. I was impressed. He did not have to utter a single word, just flick his hand like he was driving away a pesky fly and the goblins took off at a sprint. Dangling Willy did take one more look back at me. We made eye contact, and I was now certain that he was trying to make sure he got my attention.

"Since you are not marked, let me offer you a place here. If you are indeed from Portland, then you might find life out here to be very relaxing. The property is cheaper, the privacy greater, and I can offer you an army of goblins to have at your disposal."

I was actually a bit overwhelmed. How many times have you been offered an army to have at your disposal? Seriously, that is not something that just happens every day. He was giving me the real estate agent spiel on why I should move in to his territory. I have to admit, this was hands down a better offer than Morgan had ever given. Come to think of it, she hadn't really made me any sort of offer. She constantly made me seem like I was an idiot, she sent me in to situations with little or no information (case in point, I was standing here listening to another Psychic basically trying to woo me).

"What if I say no?" After all, a girl has to be aware of her options.

"Then…" the man had the decency to look hurt, "…I will allow for you to have your meeting with Merriette, and then I will require you to leave my territory. And know this, Ava Birch (wow, he knew my name), this is the only time that I will extend such an offer. There are great things in store if you join me. But, to refuse…well, that would be a foolish mistake."

"Do I get some time to think about it?"

"No."

Well, at least everything was on the table. I wish I could say that I considered his offer. The problem was more complex than I can explain, but it boiled down to the fact that there was something going on with Lisa. Also, at least with Morgan, I knew where I stood…on the bottom, and usually in the dark. There was something about this guy that gave me the creeps.

He reminded me of this old man who lived in the neighborhood that I grew up in when I was around ten or so. His name was Pete, and all the kids hung out at his house. There would be music and making out and all kinds of stuff. Of course that was back in the Seventies when nobody thought to maybe have the police go over and check things out. Of course, since I was kind of shy back then, I usually stayed on the fringe of all the activity. I seem to recall that Pete like to show certain kids his room. That was where he kept his Atari video game hooked up. I never got asked to play. Maybe I will go see if Pete is still alive when I get home.

At some point, Blue had stepped right up to me. He had a little bead of sweat on his temple. Hmm…I had never seen Morgan with a bead of sweat. In fact, until just now, I hadn't known that it was possible for her *to* sweat.

I looked Blue in the eyes and allowed Sharkmouth to come. I was really glad I could talk with Sharkmouth now, otherwise I would have sounded silly when I said, "Here is *my* offer. You send Merriette to me, I will talk with her, and then I will go. If for any reason I need to come back...I will. And if anybody tries anything, I will take it as you having sent them, and then I will find out what a Psychic tastes like."

Wow! I have no idea where Action-figure Ava came from, but she was kind of a badass. Whether it was this new ability to invoke my special powers like switchblade fingers and toes, along with Sharkmouth, or if perhaps the stress of not knowing what in the hell was going on with Lisa, I didn't care at the moment. Just now, I was feeling pretty gnarly.

"You have no idea what you are tangling with, ghoul." Blue leaned in close enough that I should be able to smell something...even if it was only his breath, but nope...still an empty space where the Psychic stood. And I guess he was done calling me by my name...I was back to just plain "ghoul."

"Yes, well I am almost willing to bet that you haven't ever tangled with a ghoul, so I could say the same to you."

"This is about the future of the Supernatural community!" Blue was shouting.

Hmm, that was another thing that made him different from Morgan. I could see all kinds of emotions on this guy's face. I saw anger...and something else. If I didn't know better, I would say it was fear. But I just could not make the leap and put this Psychic on a human level. Fear was not something that I think Morgan even remembered existed.

Personally, I was suddenly feeling really good about my choice. It was along the lines of "if it sounds too good to be true, it probably is." This guy had all but offered me the keys to my own kingdom without knowing a thing about me other than the fact that I was a ghoul.

Now, that also had me wondering just how much about myself I still did not know. I was going to absolutely hit Betty up when I got home. If she wanted me to take part in her little "thing" involving Adrianna, then she was going to have to give me more. Sure, she had already told me more about the Supernatural world in the few moments that we spoke than Morgan had in all these months, but I had a feeling that even Betty was holding out on me.

"Just go get Merriette. And no funny business."

Blue waved one hand over his head. A few second later, a cluster of goblins appeared on the far side of the little lake or pond or whatever this was that we were beside. I saw something wrapped in a silver tarp picked up and dumped unceremoniously into a paddleboat. Four goblins climbed in and the little water craft started my way. It was about halfway when it came to a stop.

"If you think I am swimming out there, you are crazy," I turned to face Blue.

"In the presence of the gods, I commend this spirit...I pray that you find it worthy," Blue had his hands raised skyward as he began to chant.

"What the—" But I didn't get to finish. I turned back to the water where all hell was breaking loose. The lake started to churn and bubble. Not like little carbonated fizzy bubbles, but huge, fit-a-car-inside-one type bubbles.

A giant figure rose from the water. I should probably give you a bit more detail. This thing was towering about twenty or so feet above the water's surface. Wet, gooey looking mud was sloughing off it and making loud plopping splashes in the lake. Since I could see perfectly in the dark, I was not bothered in the slightest as the moon ducked behind the clouds. I could still see that it was a rotten shade of brown and green. It was covered in what could be either moss or hair, and it had huge, saucer shaped eyes that were a purplish color. It did not have what I would call a nose; more like two slits that opened and closed as it breathed. Oh...and it had five or six rows of jagged teeth that looked sort of like alligator teeth.

Now, my first thought was that he was meaning me when he was talking about a sacrifice. At least until the monster reached down and scooped up the paddle boat in its hand and dumped the contents into its mouth like you might do with a box of Junior Mints.

The screams of pain were mercifully muffled as the thing chomped once or twice and then swallowed. I spun back to confront Blue, but he was gone.

Right about now, I was wishing that I had just stayed home. It would figure that, just as I was getting to understand my abilities that I was going to be eaten by a great big lake monster thingy. Life was so unfair.

And then I heard it. At first, it was almost like a whisper in the back of my mind. Only, it was...music. I will never, even if I become a much better writer (don't hold your breath on that one), be able to describe it. The best I can do is compare it to the angelic voice of Kate Bush.

Now, a lot of you might not remember Kate. Or...you just don't know the name. She had a minor hit with Peter Gabriel called *Don't Give Up*. And seriously, if you have never heard her *Hounds of Love* album...you are missing something special. But the first time I ever heard her was on a song called *Wuthering Heights*. Mariah Carey wishes she could sing that high and still sound so sweet versus annoying.

Oops...big scary monster, sorry...I was rambling.

So, here was this beast. Only, what started as a whisper became this melody that was simply beautiful. I found myself simultaneously wishing that I knew the words so that I could sing along while thankful that I didn't so that I would not screw up such an amazing sound.

I looked to my left and Aoife was slowly walking to the water's edge. She was glowing! Not in that made up way that we use to describe a pregnant woman, she was actually glowing like a pink Glo-Stick. I could see her body through the flimsy cotton dress. And, maybe it was just a trick of everything she was doing, but it almost looked like I could see the music flowing from her mouth. It carried on the breeze of her breath and began to wrap around the huge monster.

Her voice grew louder, but more like somebody turned up

the volume versus her actually singing louder. I know, this is probably not helping much, but it is the best I can do. This was some serious magic stuff. I realized in that moment just how different the Supernatural world was from the normal one that you live in. Up until this point, I think I was still looking at everything with human eyes.

You have it easy. You live in your normal world, and for the most part, you are clueless to what is going on around you. You live among monsters. Some that would just as soon eat you as not. When the sun goes down, there is a reason that something deep-rooted in your soul becomes more cautious. That voice telling you not to go down in that dark basement is there for a reason.

"Get in the car, miss," Aoife said. Only, she was still singing! I know, because I was staring right at her.

Hurry, miss, I can only hold the lake troll back for so long. This one has been kept hungry, and a hungry troll is almost as impervious to my magick as you.

Wow! She was speaking to me via telepathy! That was kind of neat. But I guess I could marvel over that later. I did not want to be lake troll chow.

I hurried to the car. My eyes were momentarily drawn to a little scratch on the hood. Oh, this Blue and his goblins were so going to pay for that...and I was not thinking of cash.

A few seconds later, the passenger door opened (on reflection, I guess I could have opened it for Aoife instead of stewing over a scratch on my car). The siren jumped in and practically collapsed. I did not wait to see if we were being followed. I had us on the road out of town in a flash.

We were winding along the coastal mountain highway heading back home. The clock readout on my radio said it was just past three in the morning. We had plenty of time to make it before sunrise.

Aoife remained silent as I drove, a true testament to how exhausted she was. In fact, she did not even grab the dash or ask me to slow down. She just remained bent over, her head actually resting on her knees. That could *not* be comfortable.

Screaming in the Night

I pulled in to the garage. And that was when I heard a second heartbeat...from my trunk.

That Ghoul Ava Kicks Some Faerie A**

6

Boom! Boom! Out Go the Lights!

"Stay in the car," I whispered to Aoife.

Of course, thinking back, that was probably a silly thing to do. I mean, if this thing in the trunk of my Corvette was a Supernatural like I expected, then it probably had exceptional hearing. That seemed to be a fairly common trait in our community. Still, there I was, thinking like a human.

I opened my car and got out, quickly bringing on Switchfingers—I didn't see the need for the toes or Sharkmouth just yet. I stopped at my trunk and listened carefully while trying to catch a good whiff. Hmm, no help there. I heard regular breathing and a heartbeat that was fluttering rather fast, but nothing was coming to the nose. Oh well, I had stalled long enough.

I thumbed my keychain remote and the trunk popped open. Staring up at me was what had to be the most pathetic looking female faerie in the world. Her hair was matted down and her skin was covered in ugly red welts. She looked up at me with pleading eyes and held her hands out as if to ward off a blow.

"You mind getting out of my trunk?" I asked, stepping back and letting my fingernails retract. I might be wrong, but I was pretty sure that I was not in any danger from this little faerie try-

59

ing anything.

"P-p-please," she stuttered, a silver tear dripped from her left eye. No, I am not exaggerating, the drop was liquid silver.

"How did you get in the trunk of my car?" I asked, still sort of strangely fascinated by that teardrop.

"One of the goblins, he slipped me away from the rest of my sisters while that horrible lake troll..." her sobs came on strong and she might have been talking still, but I was not getting a word of it.

"Okay," I tried to sound sympathetic, but something inside me just felt cold, like I was not being allowed to feel bad for this poor girl. I mean, I sensed my sympathy sort of like it was being held under a glass display case. I knew it was there, but I just could not touch it at the moment.

"It seems that you have been a busy girl," a raspy voice said from the door that led to my house.

"Hello, Betty." I didn't need to look to identify the owner. I turned to face the old woman. I took just a second to marvel that my fingers and toes had not reacted on their own. In the past, anything that gave me a start was enough to trigger my switch-fingers and toes. Apparently Betty noticed.

"Somebody has made some amazing progress since we last saw each other." Betty stepped down off the little three-step stairs that led to the door that would open to my kitchen.

"I don't know about amazing." I brushed aside the compliment, but inside, I have to admit that I was doing some serious "yay me!" cheers.

"Actually, it normally takes a ghoul a good three years to get a handle on keeping their claws under control. I've known a few that took a decade or more," Betty said with an appraising look like I was a car that she was thinking about taking for a test drive.

"Did you know that Lisa was using bits of Adrianna to wipe my memory while she was holding Templar meetings in my house?"

Okay, so I probably could have shared a teensy bit of small talk. But I was a little annoyed at some of the events of the evening. Lake trolls, goblins, and a piss poor excuse for a Psychic...you know, the typical Wednesday night.

"Yes, I taught her the incantation. Adrianna's flesh does not have the power in itself to wipe your memory, you silly ghoul." Betty waved a dismissive hand as she stepped past me to get a look at the cowering faerie.

Have you ever had somebody tell you something that caught you so far off guard, you had absolutely nothing to say. You knew about a dozen feelings that you should have felt, but instead it was just you standing there with your mouth open.

"Close your mouth, sweetie," Betty said as she actually reached over with her index finger and guided my mouth shut.

Finally, I found my voice.

"What the hell!"

I spun to Betty who was really not paying me the slightest bit of attention. She was locked on to the faerie in utter fascination.

"She needed you to be out of the loop. The Templars had to get her up to speed, and she did not feel safe meeting them anyplace else. If she met them in the house, all she needed to do was utter the word that would dispel the incantation if there was any trouble."

"Ummm...huh?"

Okay, time for an Ava break. Yes, I am doing that "breaking the third wall" thing again like Ferris Bueller. So, you would figure that I would reach some point in the story where things start to congeal. Even if it is misdirection to get you to think one thing so that I can surprise you with some sort of twist like that *Sixth Sense* director...M. Knight Shamalammadingdong or whatever his name is. For one, I really am not that clever. If you don't know that by now, then you have not been paying attention. Also, I think that might be the problem with some of those stories...life is not a dot-to-dot puzzle. It is much more like a maze drawn by a four-year-old who just polished off a six-pack of Red Bull.

Still, here is what I know about a third of the way into sharing this little adventure with you. Faeries are not under the jurisdiction of Psychics, but apparently goblins are. Also, goblins are nasty little creatures that like to run around naked, and considering the proportions of junk-to-goblin, I guess they have a right. Also, it would be hard to stuff all of that into a pair of pants. There are about five dozen variants on the troll (Aoife told me on the way home), Lisa is doing some super-secret Templar crap that I am not allowed to know about for whatever reason, but everybody else from Belinda to Betty apparently have at least some idea. Oh, and I am the talk of the Psychics in this area, but nobody seems to know that I work for Morgan.

I know that I was feeling a bit left out when I discovered that Morgan could actually claim me as one of hers—not that I wanted to be "claimed" mind you—and chose not to do so. I am starting to see the value. I do know enough about this weird world to know that the Psychics have some pretty serious territory issues that require all sorts of mother-may-I garbage. So perhaps it is best that I am seen as a free agent.

Without warning, and causing even Betty to jump, the garage door began to open. As far as I knew, only one other person besides me had a remote for my electronic garage door opener thingy.

"Lisa?"

It better be her.

"Ava, get in the house...hurry. I am pretty sure I was followed," Lisa said as she ducked in under the still-opening garage door.

Betty did not wait to be told twice. I heard her mumbling something and noticed she was reaching inside her sweater for what I can only assume to be a weapon...or maybe a wand? Aoife was right behind her with Lisa bringing up the rear. She had already pushed the button to close the garage door, but just before it shut, I thought I saw little claw-toed feet skid to a stop.

I took a moment to realize that I was now standing in my garage all alone. I decided that it was about time that I put some of my ability to the test. Instead of following everybody inside, I slipped out the door that opened to my back patio.

With a leap, I was on the roof. That was cool, and for just a moment, I wondered how high I could jump if I gave it my all…maybe later when I didn't have monsters sniffing around my garage. When I got to the front of the garage and looked down, I saw a dozen or so goblins, they were on hands and knees, sniffing around the closed door.

They were making a bunch of grunts and clicks that had me remembering some documentary that I saw once with these Amazonian tribal people. I could not pick out one single word. Okay, so eavesdropping was not going to help. Time for my second made-up-as-I-go plan.

I jumped off the roof and landed behind the little creeps. They all spun to face me, each with a weapon of some sort in his or her hand. Yeah, there were a few females in the mix. Nice to know that goblins were into the whole "equal opportunity" thing.

"I am going to give you to the count of five to get off my property," I warned. *Great, now I was sounding like that grouchy old man who always sat on his porch and told kids to get off his lawn.*

"We come for faerie…you stole faerie and want back," one of the goblins stepped forward and said.

When I say that this thing spoke, that is really stretching it. If you have seen those stupid videos where people claim that their dog is saying "I love you" or some such nonsense, that is sort of how a goblin talks. You can make out what they are saying, but you almost get the feeling that they aren't actually aware themselves and are just mimicking sounds.

Okay, back to the goblins standing in my driveway. I was having trouble with it. Not in the fact that there were actual goblins standing on my driveway; more like, how in the hell could those stubby-legged freaks get here this fast? I had driven home in my Corvette, and if you have been paying attention to my not-so-subtle comments, I am not much of a speed limit observer. There didn't seem to be any way possible that those things could get here this fast.

"You tell Blue that I have no intention of sending the faerie back with you. Consider it payment for the scratch you little freaks put on my car." All I was really hoping for was to buy some time.

The goblins all clustered together and began to chirp and click and grunt like crazy. I had zero clue what they were going on about, but it was a very animated discussion. Finally, the 'spokes goblin' turned his attention back to me.

"Who is...Blue?"

"The Psychic you little monsters work for. The one who had that lake troll eat some of your friends and that other faerie like candy? Ringing any bells?"

The goblins started in again. I wondered briefly if Rosetta Stone had a Supernatural division. Not that I would likely take the time. I had taken two years of high school Spanish and only knew a handful of naughty words and how to order at Taco Bell. A few years back, I developed this teensy crush on one of the bus boys at the restaurant where I was working as a waitress. Problem: he no *habla*. I got drunk one night and ordered Rosetta Stone after this infomercial assured me that I would be speaking like a native Spanish person in no time or my money back. (They absolutely know that over ninety percent of us will not ask for our money back. That would be admitting that we were stupid.) Oh, I have no idea if that program works or not...I think it is still around somewhere in a box. And I am also pretty sure the shrink-wrap is still intact.

"We are goblins and serve no Psychic! The only clan that weak is the Cow Fart clan by the big salt water you call the Pacific Ocean," one of the female goblins stepped forward and snarled at me.

I gave her a glance and let my claws sort of grate together. To her credit, she didn't seem to care in the slightest. In fact, she might have leaned just a little bit closer.

"So you goblins are not part of the Cow Fart clan?"

I could not believe the words coming out of my mouth. I had a Southern Belle for a grandmother. Her rule was that you had to go outside to "expel" (she could not bring herself to say the "F" word). I grew up with my own peculiar aversion to the word and had always refused to say it...apparently until tonight.

It is just a foul little word and for some reason, I probably am more embarrassed to say the word than to actually commit the act. Which, by the way, I never do in the company of others.

"We are of the Castrated Mallard clan," one of the males yipped in his odd goblin voice.

"Ava!" a voice hissed from above and behind me, "get inside, quickly!"

"Huh?"

Now, that was what I was about to say. I don't think that the word made it out of my mouth. If you have ever seen those documentaries where a bunch of ants pour over a grasshopper...well, instead of ants, it was goblins, and instead of a grasshopper, it was me.

That Ghoul Ava Kicks Some Faerie A**

7

Crackpot History and the Right to Lie

Ghouls do not sleep. We do not lose consciousness at any point, for any reason. I guess that is one of the things so prized about a ghoul. Here is a fun fact...up until recently, there had not been one single female ghoul...ever.

Way back in the old days, like, think pre-electricity—in fact, think pre-United States of America—the ghoul was a bit of a prototype for the mercenary. Because of the special skill sets of a ghoul, they were a prize to be sought.

You know what happens when someone or something gets popular? It changes into something else, usually vastly inferior. Like, for instance, the band Metallica. Listen to *Ride The Lightning*. Listen to *...And Justice for all*. Even listen to the *Black* album.

After that...it was never the same. Seriously, who writes a sequel to a song? *The Unforgiven* was good. Not great...and certainly not worth parts two and three.

Think of how stardom has destroyed so many of the child actors. The entire cast of *Different Strokes* seems to have been cursed. And would you really be surprised if you woke up tomorrow and read in the news that Danny Bonaduce went postal and died in a hail of bullets?

It seems ghouls were like the child stars of the Supernatural world way back in the Medieval Era or whatever. The reason is simple: we are perfect killers. But there is more. A ghoul has to be able to shut off certain parts of their brain. When captured, no amount of torture can make a ghoul speak. It is an established fact that if a ghoul does give up information, they do so willingly.

So, why am I sharing all of this? Because this is the extent of my knowledge of ghouls up until now. This is basically all that Betty has told me, but I am sure there is more to learn…and when I get free from this little scene, I think I am going to press her for more information.

Oh…and I am currently strapped to some big stone slab while a bunch of goblins carve on my skin, yank out my finger and toenails, and do other nasty little things that I would just as soon not share with you.

But, Ava, you the person reading this is probably saying, how can you be doing this? After all, aren't you giving your re-count of events to that ghost writer of yours? Well, yes, I am. Chantal is right here. Yeah, inside me…sort of how she possesses Lisa from time to time so we can talk. Only she can't actually possess me, because I am an undead Supernatural. However, she can sit in here like I am the Ava Auditorium and hear everything I think. And no, she can't just do that at will. She has to be given permission. Don't ask why, it's just one of the rules. Sheesh!

Right now, while those goblins are having their fun, I am in my magic Ava world. So, this is why it is so easy for my mind to wander. One thing I will look into when this is over is if I can gain some sort of control over that like I have Sharkmouth and my switchblade fingers and toes.

Just think, if I have the ability to choose when my mind wanders? That would be epic.

Hey! Is that…? Yeah, that is one of my breasts! One of those little freaks just cut it off and is sitting on my chest eating it in front of me.

That reminds me of this one girl when I was in high school.

She was the one who always had the newest clothes. And I'm not talking about just cutting off the tags. No, I mean she would have the styles and fashions that everybody else would not even know existed until like six months later. Her mom was some sort of designer. She could have been such a major bitch. But instead, she would invite her friends over when a new shipment would come, and let us pick an outfit since we were all pretty close to the same size (i.e. typical 80's version of a high school cheerleader).

That was awesome until my boobs just kept growing. I still remember that terrible February day when we went over to Cheryl Norris' house. She had new makeup still in the cases and these skirt and blouse combinations that were going to end up in a Madonna video the next month which was a guarantee that they would be super popular. Only, I couldn't get the top three buttons done on the blouse. If it had only been the last button, I could have totally rocked it. Instead, I was the only girl who did not get an outfit that day. That was also the last time I got invited over. Let me just say it here, high school girls can really be bitches.

Fun note, the Madonna video came out and she didn't have her top three buttons buttoned either. And she was wearing the cutest lacy lavender bra! I still don't know what the stupid principal's problem was that day.

So this is the upside to my tendency to let my mind wander. I keep seeing little snippets of the things that the goblins are doing to me…and I don't care. Well, that is not entirely true. I mean, I care that I am now going to be seriously lopsided, but I am only experiencing this much like you are right now. In other words, I feel more like a spectator.

Having said that, if I ever get up off this table, I am going to rip these little monsters apart. Oops, guess I don't have to worry about being lopsided anymore. *Wow, who's the hungry goblin? You are, aren't you?* Yeah, in my mind I just said that like I was talking to a puppy.

So, who was that yelling for me to get inside? People's voices always change a bit when they whisper. It's like they all become sort of generic. Sometimes, you can't even tell if it is a woman or a man. I was almost certain that this one was a man. I tried to recall if I smelt anything just prior to the warning, but nothing was coming.

Oh, wait, one of them is trying to talk to me.

"…will tell us, or the master will come and he will make you wish that you had."

"Tell you what?"

That is what I was about to ask. Funny thing, though. As soon as I started to pay attention, every single bit of the pain came in a rush and made me howl like a pissed off werewolf. The closest thing that I can equate it to is that scene in *An American Werewolf in London*. Right after they leave that inn, The Slaughtered Lamb, and then they hear that howl…yeah, about like that; but at the decibel level of an Iron Maiden concert.

Back to my happy place…back to my happy place…back to my happy place.

I have no idea how much longer I laid there being hit, poked, slapped, sliced, and other less savory things. (And trust me; there are *a lot* of less savory things.) Eventually, I realized that I was alone. The goblins had gone away.

I decided to treat my body like a swimming pool. I would dip my toe into it and see what happened. At first, I did not feel anything. So I let myself feel a bit more. It was odd, but I swear that I was controlling where I was allowing sensation to be felt. I let my awareness expand up my leg until just about the mommy part region.

I hit the brakes like a texting teenager just noticing that the light is red. Note from Ava to the kids (and stupid adults where applicable): DON'T TEXT AND DRIVE! Consider that my public service announcement. So, for those of you out there who criticized my first book or the two short stories and said that I did nothing to contribute to society…besides a great big "Duh! What did you expect from a book with *That Ghoul Ava* as the title?" Let me just give you a great big, "In your face!"

I was trying to figure out if I could just bypass that area and continue checking myself out when a bright light in the shape of a doorway appeared just to my left. One thing about having perfect vision in the dark, you can sometimes forget that you are in the dark.

"Miss Ava Birch," a voice said in greeting like we were being introduced at a formal party.

I turned my head as much as I could to get a look, but I did not see anything. Since that was a bust, I tried for a smell. Still nothing.

"You needn't bother," the voice spoke again. This time, it was as if it was right beside me, and the owner was whispering in my ear. Only...I still did not see anything.

"Why don't you show yourself," I said through clenched Sharkmouth teeth. I can't imagine that was very inviting.

"In time, little ghoul."

"What's the matter? Ya scared?" I hoped that it sounded like a taunt. That was what I was going for, but I was still having to talk through clenched teeth.

I was discovering that my ability to shut off my brain was not very effective if I was actually paying attention to outside stimulus. I needed to keep myself diverted for that special skill to work properly; apparently that was not something I could manage while actually in a conversation with somebody. Hey, don't ask me to explain the Supernatural world. In fact, if you are reading this, chances are you have been in to all that stuff for way longer than me. That means you probably have a better handle on things than I do.

"Let's just say that I am cautious," the voice said with what sounded like amusement. Also, and this was something that I was going to really try and store in my memory, the voice had what I can only call a reptilian sound to it. In other words, the 'esses' were sort of drawn out and there was a distinct lack of emotion. And I am just spit-balling this stuff. I would have said it sounded like a spider, but for one, spiders are gross little abominations that I am pretty sure were left here by aliens. And that whole 'ess' thing? Definitely something to keep an ear out for in the future. But for now, I had to try and get something from this conversation.

"Right...so basically...scared." Not a witty comeback, but I was trying to generate some sort of response.

There was a laugh that actually sounded kind of girlish. And don't go getting all worked up about how I'm being sexist. Seriously, when did it become wrong for women to be women and men to be men in this society? This laugh sounded more like it came from a teenage girl than a man, which was seriously at odds with the speaking voice...unless there were two whatever-the-hells in here with me.

"Miss Birch, I have come here to talk some sense into you. You are in way over your head and in things that do not concern you."

"How do you know what I am in?" I snapped in response. It seemed like a logical question. I mean, unless this whatever-the-hell had been following me for the past few days.

And then I got my response. Hovering just above me like a hologram being beamed by Artoo Deetoo was the image of Morgan and me at the mall having our little meeting. It was complete with audio.

I felt a few things as I watched that scene play out above me all the way up until I went down and confronted the girls and convinced them to leave. That was also when Merriette gave me the whole spiel about their sidhe being invaded and the God-mother being killed.

One of the strongest feelings that I felt was concern that something had captured this scene without either me *or* Morgan being aware. There are probably lots of Supernaturals that can duck under my radar, but I had sort of seen Morgan as totally in control of her situation at all times. This had me doubting her perfection and control just a bit. Also, I did not like how my butt looked in those pants.

"Nice trick," I said, trying to sound like I was playing it cool.

In most movies, books, and television shows, this is where the evil villain reveals his master plan. I was really hoping for that little cliché right about now, because I honestly had no clue in regards to what in the hell was going on.

"I want you to butt out of this whole faerie nonsense." The voice seemed inclined to ignore the compliment. "I want you to put all of their concerns out of your pretty little head and tell Morgan to keep her nose out as well. This is faerie business and of no concern to her or the rest of the Supernatural community."

"Yeah, well I was hired to do a job. I may have had lousy work ethics as a human, but I am trying to change. Also, a girl has to make a living. Morgan pays well. So, unless—"

"We shall double whatever your fee was for this job. Consider it a bonus for delivering our message to Morgan."

I definitely heard the "our" in there. This person or whatever-the-hell was part of something bigger. That had me wondering...

"And I also have your assurance that the faeires will not be dropping in on any more malls or other public places and turning them into public orgies? After all, that was the job I was assigned...to get the faeries to cease in their activities."

Yay for me. I was really sounding like a professional here. I have no idea where I was channeling it from. I was feeling strangely cocky and confident for absolutely no reason.

"The fey will no longer be a problem," the voice said. Only, I didn't like the way he said it.

One thing at a time, Ava, I thought. I was pretty sure that I needed to get out of here and report all of this to Morgan. Maybe she would be interested to know that another Psychic made me an offer, and that she was basically filmed meeting with me by something that she could not detect. Actually, I felt like I should be overwhelmed by all of this insanity. However, what I was mostly feeling was annoyed. And hungry.

"We will set you free. Unfortunately, that means that we will be sealing you in a steel box to transport you in order to keep this location a secret."

"Do what you have to do." Again, I was trying to sound like this was no big deal.

"And I caution you against trying to escape. It is daylight. Your kind does not fare well if exposed to direct sunlight."

"Do what you have to do." I know I was sounding like a

broken record, but the pain was really starting to trickle in through all of the cracks in my mental shield.

"We will leave you in front of your house. There are still people present there who can bring the box inside your garage once we leave."

Hmm. I didn't like that bit about them knowing what was going on inside my house. That meant that I was under surveillance as well. Somebody obviously had a pretty big opinion of my abilities.

A gaggle of goblins came flooding into the room. They wrapped these silver cords around my wrists and ankles. Of course, I was already retreating into Ava-land. That entire conversation might have seemed like no big deal to you, but you are not the one who endured a double mastectomy at the whim of a hungry goblin. And I will not detail all the other things that I was subject to, I already sort of gave you clues. If you were not paying attention, that is your fault. I understand that this is not *War & Peace*, but sheesh…try to stay with me.

Hey…I know that smell!

I do not think I had been in the box too long, and I was trying to distract myself from the pain by recalling the time that I saw Poison open for KISS. I was pretty sure that I was the *only* person there for Poison. I was thinking about how tight Brett's jeans were, and how I was really hoping that was all him and not a pair of socks. That was when I picked up on a smell that jolted me into awareness so fast that I had to bite back a scream as the pain came in a rush.

When I was about thirteen, I worked for a small pizza place. Actually, I was a dancing bear. I put on a costume that smelled like rancid sweat and handed out balloons and suckers to the little brats…err, I mean, sweet children. Sometimes, the boss would have me go outside and stand on the sidewalk, waving at all the passing cars.

That summer, I was sent to Albany, Oregon for the Timber Carnival. Basically, it is like the lumberjack Olympics if you have never heard of it. Grizzly Bear Pizza was one of the sponsors and so I was supposed to walk in the parade as a representative.

I was sent to stay with a family who managed the Albany store where I was given all the free pizza I wanted for lunch and dinner, and for breakfast, the family that I stayed with treated me to the most amazing bacon and eggs that I can ever recall. They owned a farm, and so it was all fresh. They even butchered and prepared their own pigs. Take that you meat-is-murder sissies. I was a proud carnivore way before I became a ghoul. Not that I think we need to torture them or some of the icky things they do to veal, but I am just getting sidetracked from my own sidetrack here.

But back to the smell. Albany has a paper mill. If you have never had the pleasure…just think of what your obese uncle's bed smells like after chili and pickled egg night at the local tavern. Now magnify it by ten. That is Albany. Seriously, I don't know how a town that size has a single fat person.

It was that smell seeping into my steel box. I guess real life villains are just as stupid as their fictional counterparts.

I also discovered a new trick. If I just count in my head, it works just as well as when I let my mind wander when it comes to keeping the pain at bay. I was right around five thousand four hundred and seventy-three when the vehicle I was being transported in came to a stop. I heard a bunch of claws scrabbling around and over my box. Then, I think they just shoved me out and took off. I landed pretty hard and made quite a racket.

There was a moment where I began to wonder if anybody was, in fact, at my house. And then I began to wonder if there might just be Supernaturals; most could no more come out in the sun than I could. And then I heard my door open and a handful of voices. The thing was, I only recognized one of them.

8

Voices Inside My Head

"Get that thing in the garage before the neighbors get an eyeful," Betty ordered.

"I think it may be too late for that," I heard Lisa whisper. Then her voice changed to that "nothing over here to see except a friendly neighbor" voice as she called out, "Hey there, Missus Lorence!"

"You want me to go over there and handle it?" a gruff voice that was really failing at trying to be quiet asked.

"No, Armand, I want you to just get this damn box in the garage," Betty scolded.

I tried to be calm and quiet, but for some reason I was suddenly feeling just a bit overwhelmed by my confinement. I know I'm not claustrophobic, but I can't remember wanting anything more than to be out of that stupid box.

Whoever was carrying me obviously forgot that there was a living (sort of at least) being inside the box. They dropped it unceremoniously as the automatic garage door was coming down. A moment later, the lid flipped open. I flinched, for some reason I was expecting sunlight to burn me to a crisp. Thankfully, all my titanium blinds were shut and the garage was lit by nothing more than the sixty watt bulb dangling from just above the wall-mounted tool bench that Lisa loved so much.

"Ava!" Lisa squealed, then her face peered over the lip of the steel box and her expression changed faster than those melting Nazis in *Raiders of the Lost Ark*.

I had not actually gotten a good look at myself up to this point. I had a feeling that I did not want to any time soon. Oh, and my concentration was broken; that sent the pain slamming into me again, which, in turn, made me scream at the top of my lungs.

I reached for my happy place, but with all those faces, only two that I recognized, staring down at me, I could not find it. That is probably why it went from bad to worse. I reached out for some inexplicable reason. Maybe I wanted a hug. Whatever the case, that was when I saw my nail-less fingers. That brought a new blast from my lungs. Who knew I could hit that sort of volume for so long?

This still had nothing on the time I was riding home from school in third grade and tried for the first, last, and only time to ride with no hands. My front tire caught something and turned violently and suddenly to the left. Boys, trust me when I tell you that you do not have the market cornered on bicycle-induced crotch pain.

Hey, pain gone...Ava happy. Except that just thinking about that bicycle accident gave me a dose of the heebie-jeebies. Still, I would take that in trade for the time being.

"...skin is knitting," Betty's words pulled my awareness her way for just a second.

"That is some freaky looking stuff." Lisa peered back in, however, now she was studying me like I was some sort of crazy science experiment.

"I heard that they did this, and I know that a lot of Supernaturals do something similar, but I have never seen it happen, much less so fast. Some of those injuries should take weeks to recover from...not hours," Adrianna said as she leaned in to join the others.

Wait! What is she doing out of her cell? Maybe Betty was

re-thinking her stance on how to deal with The Queen of the Zombies. Then it hit me in the stomach like a really sharp fist: HUNGRY!

I was starving!

Now, before I became a ghoul, one of my little hang-ups was hearing people say that they were starving. No, you are hungry. Starving is the poor little children in those commercials. You know, the one with the distended bellies and the flies landing on their unblinking eyeballs.

I was STARVING! It felt as if my body was eating itself from the inside out. Seeing Adrianna...no, scratch that...*smelling* Adrianna just about sent me into overload. Ava want to eat the bad lady!

I sprung.

Don't ask me how. I did not actually think that I could even move yet, much less sit up and vault from this box and pin The Queen of the Zombies to the ground. I felt my hunger seem to double as Adrianna looked up at me with surprise.

"Do it!" Betty hissed.

"Ava, no!" Lisa screamed.

The other people—or whatever they might be—seemed content to stay the heck out of it and remained quiet. Suddenly, I was Audrey Two from *Little Shop of Horrors*. It was suppertime!

The next few minutes were a blur. I don't recall anything other than the sweetest sense of satisfaction that I had ever felt in my life. This was finding a brand new pair of Jimmy Choos at a garage sale, new and in their box, for a dollar, Thanksgiving Dinner, and multiple orgasmic sex all rolled in to one.

The next thing I do actually remember is sitting on my butt against the back bumper of my Corvette while picking a piece of something from between my still present Sharkmouth teeth with one of my razor-clawed fingers. I felt a little loopy if I was being honest.

"What have you done, Ava?" Lisa was asking.

She looked really concerned. And I could see what looked like disapproval in her eyes. I did not remember at first what was going on, or even where I was at the moment. It sort of came back slowly like how the picture on my parents' television used to do back in the old days of five channels.

"Where the hell have you been," I slurred more than snapped. Then I punctuated it all with a very unladylike belch. Hey! That smelled yummy! Well at least it did to me; I thought that Lisa was going to yak right then and there.

"You just ate Adrianna!" Lisa did not answer my query, and instead chose to point out the obvious.

"I asked you a question." For some reason, I was starting to feel angry. Something was making me want to launch myself at the girl who stood over me with such disapproval. Who did she think she was, getting all high and mighty with me? It was bad enough that she joined the Templars—

In a flash, I lunged; my left hand wrapping around Lisa's throat, the long razor claws actually giving me the ability to completely encircle her slender neck.

"You left me for the Templars!" I snarled. "A group that tried to wipe ghouls off the face of the earth."

Wow, where was this anger coming from? I wondered. Not that I stopped what I was doing...I was simply curious where this rage had sprung from so suddenly.

Some garbled gibberish and a few squeaks were all I received in reply. Of course, I didn't think that Lisa could actually talk with my claw around her throat.

"Ava!" a voice spoke from behind me. Great, just what I needed.

"Not now, Morgan," I hissed. "I will have time for *you* in a minute. First, I need to deal with a certain traitor."

"You are not yourself, Ava," Morgan insisted.

"I know," I agreed, not letting my black eyed gaze leave Lisa's face for even a split second.

Lisa was a Templar. The Templars were my enemy. I must destroy my enemy. I must destroy Lisa.

That series of thoughts swirled in my head like a tornado. Only, there was something else underneath it. Something was trying to take over the destructive power that raged inside me.

The only person who I thought could do that was—

"Morgan, back off!" I roared. Whatever she was doing, I would give her this one chance to stop, or I would eat her next.

"You are experiencing the *Famé Rabbia*...the hunger rage," Morgan continued to speak. Why was she still talking? Didn't she know that she was next on my menu?

"You need to eat," Betty said from right beside me. I don't recall her being so close before. It was as if I blinked and she appeared.

I looked around to discover that I was in my sound proof basement. And where was Lisa? Hadn't I just seen her a moment ago?

A body was on the stainless steel table in front of me just waiting to be consumed. Ooo, and this was relatively fresh. It could not have been dead for more than an hour or two. And he was kind of cute. So sad when somebody so young dies. This guy looked like he was not much older than Lisa.

Lisa!

And in another blink I was sitting on the table, Hadn't there been a meal...err...I mean corpse here just a moment ago?

"That's five," a voice said from the top of the stairs. "You think she is...normal yet?"

"Lisa?" I craned my neck so I could look up the stairs at the source of the voice. Did she just flinch?

"Ava?" Lisa sounded strange...almost like that first night that we met when she was—

"Are you afraid of me?" I asked, climbing down off the table. That's strange, it was kind of messy. I never left a mess when I fed. Wait! When did I feed?

"Glad to see you looking better, Miss Birch," a voice that was not at all familiar, yet very, spoke from nearby. This is making my head hurt.

I spun to face the source of the newest voice and instantly called upon my fangs, fingers, and toes. I had no idea how, but a goblin was standing in *my* basement. This would be like the Joker showing up in the Batcave.

Mmm, Heath Ledger. No! Bad Ava! Focus!

"What is *that* doing in my home?" I pointed at the goblin in disgust like I would if somebody had pooped on my carpet…on purpose.

"That might take some explaining, and we will get to it soon enough." Morgan came down the stairs. She wasn't exactly showing any expression, but she seemed different somehow. Like she was—

"No way!" I blurted. "You can't be scared of me too!"

"I would hardly say that I am *scared* of you, Ava," Morgan snorted with a dismissive wave of her hand. Only…there was something different. She was not exactly telling the truth. I don't know how I knew, but I did.

"I see she has finally settled down," another voice drifted past Morgan and Lisa.

"Hey, Betty," I said with an absent wave as my mind felt like it was shifting in my head.

I was starting to remember something. It was like the Tasmanian Devil. Only, I was looking through his eyes and he was no longer the cute cartoon. Instead, he was a whirling dervish of blood and gore and meaty bits.

"What is Fa…may…umm…Rabies? Famay Rabies? Is that it?"

"*Famé Rabbia*," Morgan corrected. "It is a state of crazed hunger that can come to a ghoul when they are lacking the sustenance that they need. It is most often brought on when they have suffered horrible injury."

I whirled on the goblin. "You!"

I suddenly recognized this one. Sure, for the most part, all goblins looked alike as far as I was concerned. And don't get all prissy. If you ever see a group of goblins, I defy you to pick one from the other. So I'm not being a ghoul supremacist or anything else that may be crossing your mind.

This was the goblin with an attitude that I had encountered when I ran in to Blue. He was the one that kept giving me the dirty looks. But, there was a faerie in my trunk…and then these other goblins…I was getting more confused by the second.

"Somebody mind telling me what the heck is going on?" I

snarled, not taking my eyes off of the goblin.

And make sure they eventually get to me! a familiar voice spat.

I looked around. I know I had heard Adrianna, but I did not see her anywhere. That was strange.

And perhaps you could figure out a way in that ghoulish brain of yours to shelter me from some of your more mundane thoughts.

I looked around. It was almost like Adrianna was in my head! A memory broke free. I was ripping through Adrianna like Cartman on a bucket of KFC. Okay, I realize that some of you might not get that reference. I was trying to be polite, but you know what? That's just not me. I had torn in to Adrianna like a fat kid on a candy bar. There, you get it now?

With one slash from my finger claws, I had severed her head and stuffed it into my mouth in a single bite. It was like one of those chocolate covered cherries that you always see around Christmas; so sweet and yummy, with a filling that burst in my mouth with a wave of flavorful pleasure. I made short work of her, hardly bothering to savor just how splendidly delicious every single bite tasted.

In that flash of memory, I recall Betty standing just out of reach. She was muttering something that was probably Latin, or that "ubby-dub" language they used to sing on the show *Zoom*. Lisa was trying to say something, but Morgan was keeping her back and telling her to stay quiet. There was a moment when my vision shifted to Lisa, and in that instant, I saw a type of fear expressed by another person that I'd never witnessed in my life. Those Hollywood "scream queens" have nothing compared to what I saw etched on Lisa's face. I was really hoping that my memory was flawed. I would never want anybody to look at me like that and mean it.

"Why do I hear Adrianna's voice in my head?" I asked. My gaze shifted to Betty. "And what in God's name is a goblin doing in my basement?" Honestly, don't those seem like perfectly logical questions; just not ones that you would ever imagine asking out loud.

"The sentence of The Queen of the Zombies has been carried out," Betty and Morgan said together.

And when in the hell did these two meet each other? Betty was supposed to be my ace-in-the-hole to use when Morgan was being a snot. Now they were talking in unison like creepy twins?

"Okay…?" I waved my hands in that universal gesture that means "Keep talking, you ain't done 'splainin' yet."

"You and I have already come to an agreement that you would take part in the final punishment of Adrianna," Betty said with a bit of an attitude.

"Okay." I nodded. "But that does not explain why I am hearing her voice in my head."

Oh, this is priceless, Adrianna crowed from somewhere right behind my right eyeball.

"And you shut up!"

"I see that you and her are now linked. We were actually only partially sure that this would work," Morgan said.

"Speak for yourself," Betty harrumphed.

"What do you mean when you say that me and The Queen of Bitches (and I spoke those word with capital letters) are linked?"

"You have absorbed her being into your own," Betty said. I glanced at Morgan. I may have been imagining, but I am pretty sure that Morgan was trying to wave the old lady off like a plane coming in to a bad runway.

"And so now I have to listen to her bitch and moan whenever she gets a bee in her bonnet?" I asked.

Actually, I had some other rather flowery but derogatory things I wanted to say, but I didn't want to fire all my guns early and have nothing in reserve. To say that I was unhappy with this newest development would have been putting it mildly. And then Betty spilled the beans and made everything all better.

"You can partition her off whenever you like. It is like any other skill that you learn, it will not be perfect, but if you shut her away for extended periods, I imagine she will learn to play nice. Also, you have absorbed a very powerful Supernatural. While I certainly won't be able to guess the extent, this usually comes with some residual power benefits for the ghoul." Betty actually made it sound kind or boring. It was like she was a second grade teacher doing her best not to sound uninterested while sharing the concept of basic math.

I mulled over what she said for a moment. I could tell by the look on Morgan's face that she was not exactly thrilled that Betty was being so helpful. That had me more puzzled than annoyed. Why would she not want me to know about any special powers that I may or may not have at my disposal? After all, she was the one using me to keep her streets clean, so to speak.

"Are you saying that I could make zombies?" I blurted. That was probably not the best question to ask. I am sure that Adrianna had lots of other powers that would not have such an "I want to bring about the end of the world" sound to them.

Actually, since I can be honest with you because of this whole "you think this is just cheesy fiction" thing going on at your end, my real thought was that zombies are super yummy and give me just a bit of a buzz. It would be like having my own ability to make all the booze I could drink.

Leave it to you to turn such an amazing ability into something so base and crass, Adrianna muttered.

I tried to get my brain around the idea of putting her in a quiet little room in my mind. That only brought on more of her snide derision and biting remarks.

You want to pen me up in here and can't figure out where? she said with a Wicked Witch of the West sort of laugh. *Considering all the vacant space, I hardly think you should find a problem.*

"Are you going to be this way all the time?" I asked.

Betty, Morgan, Lisa, and even the goblin were looking at me funny. I pointed to my head.

"Talking to Adrianna…sorry about the confusion."

Your ignorance is laughable.

I decided to try something. In my head, I screamed as loud as possible. Funny thing about that; you don't need to catch your breath. After about a minute, I stopped.

"…has important information about this whole faerie nonsense…" Morgan was talking. Oops.

That is quite enough! Adrianna snapped.

Or what, I thought back. *Here is how things are going to work. You are going to hush, and we will work out the details of your living arrangement later.*

With that, I ignored Adrianna and turned all my focus to Morgan…who was still speaking.

"…and if this is true, then this could signal a shift in power so massive that the Templars will have no choice but to lump all Supernaturals together and commence an extinguishment plan."

"So…bad stuff," I said with a nod.

I glanced at Lisa who rolled her eyes. I think she knew that I had missed some, most, or even all of what Morgan was telling me. I also knew in that moment that I could trust her. Whatever had happened at the mall was something that had nothing to do with our relationship. She would tell me or she wouldn't, but I had to believe that Lisa was my friend. If I didn't, then I was truly alone. I felt more than heard a bit of a grumble in my head.

"If this Prince Fraylee is working with goblins and is in fact teaming up with a renegade Psychic, then—"

"Blue!" I blurted. Hmm, I'm starting to make a habit of the whole blurting thing…I should probably try to pull it back a little.

"May his insides turn to rotten jelly and ooze from his skin," the goblin said and then spat on the floor of my garage.

"Hey!" I snapped. "You get a rag and wipe that up!"

The goblin looked at me like we suddenly had a language barrier. He shot a questioning glance down to the green and brown wad on the smooth concrete floor of my garage. I nodded.

"Then where shall I spit my curses if not on the ground?" he asked like that question made perfect sense.

"You do what you want outside or in your home, but in my house…no spitting!" Many a man has cheered that policy in the past.

"Is this really the time, Ava?" Lisa asked as she came down the rest of the stairs and joined our small cluster.

"Miss Birch has some serious catching up to do," Betty said,

86

steering me towards the stairs that led to the main part of the house. "I suggest we stop all of this nonsense for now." She fixed her gaze on me. "And you will undoubtedly have many questions. Once this particular threat is dealt with, we can address them, but for now, you need to get your mind back on the job."

"As I was saying," Morgan resumed her authoritative posture and gave everybody in the room that look of hers that, while seeming to lack any expression at all, makes you feel properly scolded. "If Prince Fraylee has turned on his own people and is working with the goblins, there has to be a reason. It has not been a secret that the prince was angry after his sister rose to the position of Godmother. He had spent centuries courting Lady Simone in hopes that he would share the throne with her."

"Hold on," I interrupted. "This is all sounding like a bad soap opera."

"Be that as it may," Morgan continued, not even taking the time to shoot me a dirty look, "the prince was banished about a hundred years ago. There were a lot of rumors as to where he vanished, but nothing could ever be confirmed. Those rumors only grew when the faerie and goblin war began. Many believed that it was the prince's doing. The Templars went in to mediate, but nothing was resolved. The decision was made to revoke any and all access to any weapons that could be lethal to either side. The Templars actually believed, as did most everybody, that the two sides would get tired of the conflict after a decade or two."

That Ghoul Ava Kicks Some Faerie A**

9

You Got Another Thing Comin'

I was still not entirely sure that I had a grip on what was going on. Here are some of the high points that Betty and Morgan decided to share with me. First, this *Famé Rabbia*; it was brought on because of all the damage that I took during the torture at the hands of the Castrated Mallard goblin clan, may they all burn. (Huh, what do you know? I had to fight the urge to spit. Stupid goblins.)

According to the Dynamic Duo, a ghoul can come back from just about anything. And here is a real kicker, we are practically fire proof! I know, how crazy is that? All firemen should be ghouls, that way we would not have any more of those terrible and sad tales of such heroic people coming to such dreadful endings. Of course, then the public would probably insist that they all get minimum wage. They would be treated worse than teachers in public schools. Oops, sidetracking…sorry.

Anyways, as I was saying, unless it is from a specially designed weapon that you can only get from Cold Steel, nothing done to me causes permanent physical damage. And yay! The twins were back where they belonged! Sheesh, glad I wasn't a virgin before the turn…that would suck. The downside is that my body craves energy, and the only way I can get it is to eat. This is where some ghouls got a bad reputation. I guess we are not in our right state of mind during the *Famé Rabbia*. While it is a fact that we only eat the dead, from what they both told me as well as the somewhat disturbing video playback that they showed me, we are not above helping people reach that state while that whole mess is happening.

As far as the situation with the faeries, this is where it gets complicated. The faeries and the goblins have been sort of at war with each other for around a thousand years or so. Things were kept between the two, so there was no need for the rest of the Supernatural community to really be involved. That changed when—and this is according to Rain, the faerie that was in my trunk—a Templar took up arms with a goblin raid and helped to basically wipe out over two-thirds of the sidhe, including the Godmother who also happened to be Merriette's mom.

Okay, when I say "war", that could be stretching things a bit. I guess, up until just recently, these battles were non-lethal. There was plenty of fighting, but since nobody had any special weapons, none of the battles ended with a single fatality.

To their credit, the goblins say—and this is based on what Nose Wart (I know, who names their kid that?) the spitting goblin currently in my house is telling us—that they were not aware the weapons they were using that night had come from a Cold Steel facility. Of course the faeries are not buying any of it and insist that the goblins have been upping the battles recently because of their desire to introduce faerie blood into their genealogy.

For me, the bit that stands out is the fact that a Templar is being named. Of course Lisa says that it would be impossible for a Templar to do such a thing because it violates several of their secret little codes. I don't think she pays much attention to the news; people in charge are always doing something shady.

The problem on the goblins' side of this is that they don't have a name (not that whoever this is, if he is actually a Templar, would give his real name). It does not help that they are sort of known as liars and cheats. In fact, according to Morgan and confirmed by Nose Wart (really trying not to laugh every time I say his name), goblins earn status in their clan by pulling dirty deals amongst their clan. I have no idea how they manage to do any business without just killing each other. I mean, can you even begin to imagine going to a market when you know that the vendors take pride in how much they can get from you while giving you as little for your money as possible? Wait...did I just describe malls?

"I guess we have our work cut out for us," Lisa said after everything was laid out on the table so to speak.

"We?" a chorus consisting of me, Morgan, and Betty all said in unison.

"You can't be involved in this one," I said. "We still have not talked about your little disappearing act the other night. I realize this might hurt your feelings, but I just don't know how much I can trust you."

"Of course there is the whole thing about a Templar possibly being at the root of the problem," Betty said with a bit of an attitude creeping in to her voice.

"Yeah...that too," I agreed. "But I'm not willing to paint her with that broad of a brush yet...to say that she can't do something just because another Templar might be dirty? Did you ever stop to think that perhaps somebody might be trying to set the Templars up to look bad?"

Judging by the look on both Betty's and Morgan's faces, they hadn't. I think they were looking at this with much different eyes than I am. They have centuries of history with the Templars. I have less than a year as a Supernatural. I guess I have not had time to get as jaded. Now don't get me wrong, I have been learning about the history and I know that the Templars tried to exterminate all ghouls, but I also know that Americans owned slaves a couple of hundred years ago or so. That does not mean that every American is evil...just the bigots, racists, bankers, lawyers, and politicians.

"All the more reason that you should bring me with you," Lisa insisted.

"I can't wait to hear this," Betty quipped as she leaned back in the recliner like she was settling in for a good (or at least long) movie.

"If there is a Templar involved, then the Circle needs to know," Lisa insisted.

"Unless the person we discover just happens to be a member of this little Circle," I offered.

Seriously, in the movies it is always the leader of whatever super-secret organization is in question who decides to make a grab for more power. People are never satisfied with having lots...they always want more.

"And again, since I have the background, I would know," Lisa pointed out.

"I believe I am quite a bit more familiar with the upper echelon of the Templars," Morgan said with her usual lack of emotion. "I see you as a liability on this mission. And this is not just another one of those instances where I would prefer that you not be involved because I don't want you privy to secrets of the Supernatural community, it is—"

"Wait...what?" I interrupted. "Are you saying that the reason up to now that you didn't want Lisa with me had nothing to do with concern for her safety? That is was solely because you did not want a mortal human discovering trade secrets?"

"As usual, you are simplifying things to a level of your minimal understanding." Morgan turned to face me. "You have no idea how complex this world is, Ava Birch. You treat everything like it relates to humans. Your inexperience and youth is dangerous and compounded by your lack of understanding."

Wow, she was not holding anything back. Well, if she thought I was just going to sit here in my house and take it without giving any in return, she had another thing coming.

"Well maybe I would make better choices and decisions if I actually knew what was going on other than being pointed in a direction and shoved out the door!" I snapped. "In just the short time we have been associating with each other, you have sent me out as bait for a power hungry vampire so that none of your precious fanged pals like...hmm...Belinda, would be in danger.

"You sent me after The Queen of the Zombies without

bothering to warn me that her status of actually being undead would make her like ghoul crack, and that she could use her powers of control over me. In fact, it was that hag Belinda that told me Adrianna caused the freakin' Black Plague..."

Ah yes, the good old days, Adrianna sighed. Apparently I could not keep her blocked off when I was super emotional. And right now, I was building up a head of pissed off steam. I'd had about enough of Morgan.

"You don't even bother to claim me in your territory," I continued my rant. "And do you know what kind of offer I received from one of your fellow Psychics? He was set to give me a house and my very own goblin army without even a moment's hesitation."

"And is that what you want, Ava?" Morgan still sounded her usual unemotional self, but I think I saw a slight pinching around the eyes. "Do you need little pats on the back with me telling you what a good girl you are? And seriously, a goblin army? What would you do with a goblin army? Do you have any idea how much it costs to keep them fed? My guess is that he was very aware of just how new and naïve you happen to be. He was probably trying to get out from under having to care for the goblins and saw you as the perfect opportunity."

"Of course, it couldn't be that he valued me and wanted to reward my greatness and ability with something fitting." *Yeah, when I look at that statement, it does seem a bit shallow and egotistical.*

"Nose Wart?" Morgan turned her head to the goblin and fixed the little vermin with her gaze. I thought the tiny thing was going to fall over and die! "If you are in service of another...say if your clan were to become my own personal army, who becomes responsible for your clan and its proper care?"

"Umm..." I could tell old Nose Wart was wishing that he could vanish. "Well, Psychic Morgan, we would become your responsibility."

He said the word "Psychic" like you might use "Doctor". It was obviously being used as a title.

"If you are given a clan of goblins, you are completely responsible for them from that moment on," Morgan said. If I didn't know better, I would swear she had a bit of a gloat going on. "You can barely manage your funds with just you and Lisa. Most people could not spend in a year what you spend in a month. And before you say a word, don't think I have not tracked your book sales since you started putting them out. Were you not receiving jobs from me, you would be so impoverished that you could not afford to pay attention."

Wait! Did Morgan just crack a joke?

"My books do okay," I grumbled.

Of course that was a lie. If I wrote personal thank you letters to everybody that had purchased a copy of the first full-length one, well, I would probably still have the same box of thank you cards on my desk with a few left over. I barely made enough money to buy a single bottle of the stuff that Lisa sprays on my body with an airbrush anytime I want to go out and be around humans. Heck, I couldn't scrape all the money together and buy the glasses that I wear to hide my all-black eyes.

"They do dismally. And that poor girl you have producing them for those too lazy to read…you must have pictures of her performing something illegal for her to agree to spend the time it takes to read through your drivel and make it at least sound interesting for her to do so for the money she has been paid."

So now Morgan is channeling Don Rickles? And if you don't know who that is…you have my sympathy. For those who think people like Howard Stern is so controversial, they got nothing on old man Rickles. You might know him better as Mister Potato Head from *Toy Story*. He was insulting people in his act back when a lot of stars may or may not have had actual mob connections. And he didn't care.

Still, Morgan had a point. The books were something that I was really only doing as a hobby. It seemed that, while I did have a bit of a following, it was pretty small. Like…they could all fit around my dinner table small. I sure wasn't making enough to live off of with them. I certainly was not raking in what it would take to feed an army…even if it was just an army of goblins. Seriously, how much could one of those little buggers eat?

"So your argument about how quickly you were appreciated by Blumegastrickfiggernilly is moot." Morgan paused and I swear that I saw her lips curve up just a bit. Then she zinged me again. "That means pointless. That particular word is not on your calendar for another two weeks."

"Yeah, well..." I felt my tongue twist into a knot. Okay, maybe it didn't literally do that, but it sure felt like it all of a sudden.

"I have been showing you my appreciation in the manner in which I felt you would most benefit...in other words, money. That flea bag of an apartment that you were residing in when we first became acquainted was leaking sunlight in from everywhere. You were practically pinned down in your bedroom closet. And now you have all of this." She waved her arms around to encompass my amazing home.

I thought it over. She had done a pretty good job at countering my main argument about her not showing me any appreciation. And then it hit me, she had completely dodged the bit about almost getting me killed and being so stingy with information. But, before I could point that out to her, she let me have it with the other barrel.

"And as for this ridiculous claim about endangering *your* life, ghouls are practically impossible to kill. Also, it is common knowledge that a ghoul learns their skill set under situations of duress. The best way to get you suited for your position was to toss you into the lake and make you swim, if I might steal a comparison to a common parental swimming lesson example."

So there I stood with my mouth open. She had pretty much sunk my primary complaints with what, at least on the surface, seemed like logical explanations. I should have known that she was not quite done.

"And the reason that I did not, nor will I ever, *claim* you, is due to the fact that a ghoul is able to operate best without being marked as being in the service of another. Sure, it leaves that ghoul open to pursue other offers, but I gave you enough credit to believe that you possessed some degree of loyalty."

Ouch. Just like that, Morgan had gone from being the jerk to the good guy in this little scene. I was feeling kind of small. Well, until Lisa stepped up to the plate.

"All that crap might work on Ava," Lisa said with some serious venom in her voice. "However, I think you are full of bull. You have thrown Ava out there unprepared time and time again. And I don't want to hear about how a stressful situation brings out a ghoul's abilities. You could have told her about how to use her mind, but instead, you made it a point to belittle her every single time she wandered of mentally. And as for her being invincible? Were we looking at the same person inside that box? She was in absolute agony! I have never seen pain like that? What was that supposed to teach her..."

The human has spunk, I don't believe that any human, Templar or otherwise, has ever spoken to Morgan like that, Adrianna said with genuine appreciation. *Perhaps if I would have focused more of my attention on her, I would have been victorious. It is clear where the brains of this little team reside.*

You know, I made sure to shout as loud as I could in my mind, *you were doing fine until that last statement. I thought I could let you out of your box. I see that I was mistaken.*

As I worked to put Adrianna in her place, I was able to actually resume listening to Lisa. She was still pretty fired up.

"...when you suggested that I become a Templar? You and I both know that it was to suit your needs. And I am almost willing to bet that you started making plans for how you could use me once Ava and I split up. You had to know that a Templar and a ghoul could not live under the same roof. Well I have news for you, our friendship is a lot stronger than you think. She saved me from who knows what kind of life. And then she made me get my GED..."

Oh yeah. I had almost forgotten about that. When she told me that she hadn't graduated, I let her know that she could do whatever she wanted after she finished school. I even hinted that there might be her very own car involved.

"...and when I told my trainer from the Templars, he said that he fully supported that endeavor. In fact," Lisa turned to face me with the kookiest grin I'd ever seen, "let's put one big mystery to bed right now.

"The night you met Morgan and things went crazy in the mall? I had totally forgotten that I had my final test that night. I got a text from Race Mitchell, he is sort of like my mentor, but he has also been tutoring me in math.

"If you show up late for the test, they won't let you in…not even if you are just five minutes late. So, we were in a hurry. He practically pulled me into the van while it was still moving."

Okay, that seemed sensible. And that was another mouse in the house solved. What? You don't know about the "mouse in the house" theory. Oh, you are missing out on one of my ex-boyfriends all-time great male leaps of logic. He explained how a gal telling her boyfriend that there is a mouse in the house while on the phone with him could be turned in to she is having an affair.

Are you ready for this one? Oh don't be such a butt, it is not like the story is going to go anywhere. And no, this is not one of my "spaced out Ava" moments that a few of you found annoying. And yes, Mary in Kansas, I do know that they have medication for that, thank you very much; but now, back to the "mouse in the house" theory.

So, a guy calls his girl just as she is walking in the house with groceries. Just after she answers, a mouse scurries in the door. Don't ask me why, I didn't make up this theory. The conversation and inner-thought process goes something like this:

"Hold on a second, babe, there is a mouse in the house."

Mouse in the house? the boy thinks. *Why is there a mouse in the house? Did she leave the door open? Why would she leave the door open, she never leaves the door open? She must have somebody with her and was going to let them shut the door. Somebody is with her. If it was one of her friends, they would have yelled "hello" in the background like they always do. Whoever is with her does not want me to know he is there. A guy is in my girlfriend's house.*

"You cheating whore!"

See? Mouse in the house. Lisa being pulled in to a van,

while certainly not something you would expect every day, has a very reasonable and logical answer. While there were still some things she and I needed to hash out, her being my friend was certainly not one of them.

"Aren't you going to ask me how I did?" Lisa was looking at me expectantly.

"I am going to assume that you passed based on the fact that you are asking me to guess," I answered with a smile and that nod thing we do when we expect people to agree with us.

"Better!" Lisa reached in her pocket and pulled out a long four foot piece of rope. When I continued to stand in ignorance-based silence, Lisa explained. "If your score averages are above a seven hundred and fifty, you graduate with honors and get to wear this gold cord with your cap and gown during graduation."

Since I was never much better than a "C" student, I was not going to diminish Lisa's accomplishment. I know some folks look down on a GED, and maybe it isn't a high school diploma, but it took self-determination to pass. And not only did she pass, but she did so with honors.

"Yay for you!" I exclaimed and swept her up in a big hug.

"And all of this is wonderful...really," Morgan interrupted. "However, we still have some very pressing issues that could be a threat to the entire Supernatural community."

"And I will be involved," Lisa insisted.

I saw the entire scene starting over again. You don't want to read it, and I didn't want to live it.

"Fine," I said. "Lisa goes with Betty. You two need to go talk with whoever Lisa can get to listen over at Templar Secret Headquarters or the Hall of Justice, or whatever it is that you guys call your meeting place. I think you need to start with finding out just exactly who was in on that mediation. Perhaps they can shed some light.

"Morgan, you just do whatever it is that you do. I will take Rain and Nose Wart." I stifled another giggle. Sorry, some things just strike me as funny. "We are going to poke around in the old sidhe as well as see about talking to anybody that can lead us to Prince...what did you say his name was?"

"Fraylee," Morgan said with a drawn out slowness. "And what exactly makes you think that you will be able to locate the prince when nothing else has worked over the years?"

"Well, that is why you hired me," I said with a shrug. "I just find a way to get the job done…even if it is completely by accident."

I don't think that offered her any sort of consolation, but that was my best answer. I headed towards the door, but stopped when Morgan cleared her throat. I paused and turned to see what she had her panties in a bunch over this time.

"Unless you also have gained the ability to endure the sunlight, perhaps you should wait for a few hours."

I hadn't thought of that.

That Ghoul Ava Kicks Some Faerie A**

10

The Waiting

We did not waste the time as we waited for darkness. Actually, it was only me and Nose Wart who were truly trapped indoors. Goblins turn to mud in the sunlight…good to know.

I decided that Rain could get me up to speed on this Prince Fraylee individual. The hard part was actually paying attention. Lisa was not yet done with Morgan and those two went off someplace to talk. The Psychic must have a few tricks up her sleeve because I could not hear a word.

And I wasn't done with Lisa yet either. I wanted to know what the hell kind of meetings she was having in my house that required she slip me the Supernatural equivalent of Rohypnol (that is one of the more common date rape drugs for those of you scratching your head). And why were Templars being allowed to stomp around and become familiar with where I live? That would be like handing the blueprints of your fortress to the enemy. Which also reminded me, I was going to need to invest in some pretty heavy duty security.

Betty was down in the basement. She told me that she was going to get rid of the extra-dimensional jail cell that had housed Adrianna. When I told her that it might not be a bad idea to keep it in place—never knew what sort of terrible creature I might encounter—she agreed and said that she could instead go down and boost the detainment capabilities. Whatever made her happy.

As for all the other strangers who had been present, they all moved to various locations both outside (which meant they were human and not vulnerable to the sun) and in. I guess Betty had her own security force that she could summon when she needed. I only briefly wondered why she did not do so when Adrianna first popped in and snatched up her mortal husband for zombie practice.

Betty marches to her own drum, Adrianna offered. *You would be wise to always keep an eye on her.* I ignored the remark. I was not going to dismiss it, but I was also not going to let her turn me into a paranoid basket case.

"The prince is rumored to have bred with his choice of goblin females..." Rain was simply rambling on about any rumor she had ever heard.

I had told her that it did not matter how far-fetched the rumor was, if she'd heard it, I wanted her to spill it. So far, none of what she had said sparked even the tiniest interest from me. At least until now.

"Wait, why would he want to breed with a goblin?"

I really can't convey just how vile looking the little freaks are; and I have so far avoided discussing their smell for the most part. I can't vouch for a human nose, but to me, they are a mixture of rotten eggs dipped in spoiled cabbage and then heated to about three hundred degrees.

"Sometimes the mutated spawn of faerie and goblin will survive," Rain said. She was looking at me like I should just understand. Then she shook her head and sighed. "I apologize. I forget that you are not familiar. Your Psychic really should lend you a copy of the *Unnatural Grimoire*."

I bet your mind automatically flashed on some evil looking book wrapped in human flesh with a blood-stained binding. Well I know that mine did. Turns out it is more like a set of encyclopedias. And you can actually order them from Amazon.su.com.

The Waiting

What? You don't think that retail portal hasn't found a way into the Supernatural market? And they even have the series for my Kindle. Of course I would not have the time to read all dozen volumes. And at a thousand or so pages each, I probably never would. I only say probably because, if I live for hundreds of years, I might get around to it. This set of books has entries on every known type of monster in the Supernatural community.

Hmm, I bet you are wondering the same thing that I am. Why wouldn't Morgan want me to know about or have such a thing? Yeah...me too.

Of course, these books are pretty spendy, even for a Super-natural. They run a cool hundred million. I know! Also, according to Rain, you are listed on some sort of register when you buy the set. So basically like the human equivalent of *Catcher in the Rye* if you believe in the urban legend. And con-sidering that Rain said Morgan should "lend" me her copy...I am making the logical assumption of at least one name on that registered owners' list.

Anyway, back to the mutated spawn of faeries and goblins. Some of the better known creatures are trolls! Now, just who do I know that hangs out with goblins and happens to have a troll apparently working for him?

Some of the other creatures include bugbears—nasty crea-tures that stand about eight feet tall and look like the Gizmo character from *Gremlins* but have a real hunger for fresh meat; and there are others, some with wings, a few that live in water. Loch Ness mystery? Solved. Hey, you don't have to believe me. Actually, it is better if you don't. Besides, you humans don't ev-er want to really know what lurks in the dark. Trust me, though, it is way worse than that creepy guy two houses down.

"Okay, I know this is probably a stupid question, but would these mutations as you call them be covered under the treaties or agreements or whatever exists between the Supernatural com-munity and the Templars? And would they fall under the jurisdiction of a regional Psychic?"

Rain considered my question with a look of deep thought on her face. How she could look so amazingly beautiful by doing something as simple as thinking was just another mystery. If I think too hard on a subject, I usually just look constipated. However, it was not Rain who spoke up with an answer.

"No," Nose Wart said. He cowered back from me a step when I turned my attention his direction. I guess I really hadn't been that nice to him up to this point.

"Give me more than just the word 'no' for an answer, Nosey," I said, trying to sound at least a little friendly. Hey, I even gave him what I thought was a cute nickname. Judging by his scowl, I do not think he cared for it much.

"These mutations, as the faeries refer to them, do not have a part in the agreement with the Templars. They technically do not exist. They are not acknowledged, nor are they given a say in anything to do with their own lives. They are born and become servants or...pets, yes, that would be a good word and way to describe them."

Nose Wart was actually pacing back and forth as he spoke, his hands or claws or whatever those things at the end of his arms could be called, were clasped behind his back. All he needed was a set of bifocals and he would be the Professor Nose Wart.

"And why have they not been added in to the agreement with the Templars?" Again, that seemed like a logical question.

"They are non-beings," Nose Wart answered with a simple shrug. "They are nothing and live only at the pleasure of whatever goblin clan they are born in to. As far as any Psychic bothering to claim one, that would be like you going outside and claiming a passing dung beetle."

I must have had one of my confused looks, because Nose Wart paused and dropped his chin to his chest for a second like he was trying to come up with something that actually made sense.

"Miss Birch...may I call you that?" Nose Wart asked with a tentative pause.

"Just Ava is fine," I said with a wave of my hand.

"As you wish, Just Ava. I heard Morgan express some concerns that you still think as a human. You are doing that here. In the world of the Supernatural, the ways are simply not relatable in many cases. Humans are silly creatures that obtain pets and then talk to them as if they understood. Humans pay money for chicken when there are plenty of those tasty snacks just sitting in wooden buildings with fences that require almost no effort to get over. They wear clothing that is far too restricting and then ask others if it makes them look fat. Humans seek out other humans based on ridiculous things like how they look when time will eventually equalize them all with wrinkles and thinning hair."

"Okay. Mister Smarty Goblin, if Supernaturals are so much better, then what does a goblin look for in a mate?"

He looked at me like I was crazy. Heck, maybe I was. Here we were trying to stop a Supernatural genocide and I was asking about goblin dating preferences.

"Taste, then smell, then fighting ability," Nose Wart ticked off on his finger claws.

"Taste?" My mind (and yours I'm sure) went straight to the gutter.

"Yes, before a goblin would even consider a courting ritual, a small piece of flesh is offered. After all, who else would eat you if you die?" He made that last statement like it was so perfectly natural. And based on my diet, who was I to judge? "If the recipient finds it pleasing, he or she will offer a piece in return.

"As for smell, on the first night of the courting ritual, the couple will spend an hour or so sniffing the other from head to toe."

I tried to picture any of my dates ending that way. Nope. Not even right out of the shower. Sorry, but a butt is still a butt no matter the scrubbing.

"And last, in the event of an attack, every goblin is expected to defend the warren. It does not matter that we live in a time of relative peace, there can never be a moment when we are not ready for the final battle as promised in the scrolls from our ancestors."

Every society has an apocalypse theory…why not goblins?

Okay, so now I knew about goblin dating preferences. I still was not sure what point he was trying to make.

"Just Ava…"

Wait, was he actually calling me "Just Ava" as my name?

"…you have only been part of us for a short time. I have often heard tales of ghouls in those early years. Actually, most never live long enough for their names to be remembered. You are not the first to struggle with discarding your human ways. However, I can assure you that failing to do so will end poorly for you. You think in a way that no longer is relevant…"

Okay, not to point it out, but this goblin was talking like Morgan. I mean, looking at him, I would not expect him capable of this sort of reasoning. Goblins all seem like nasty, vicious little beasts. Wait…is this part of my problem?

Crap. I am still seeing *them* as monsters. That is coming from somebody who has gray skin, solid black orbs for eyes, claws that are like switchblade knives that come from my fingers and toes, and a mouth that more than quadruples in size and sprouts three razor sharp rows of needle-like fangs that can chew up an entire human corpse in less that fifteen minutes.

My name is Ava Birch. I am a ghoul. I am a monster.

"Okay!" I raised my hand to silence Nose Wart. "I get it. I need to embrace my inner-monster. So let's get back to the main issue. What would some faerie be doing living with goblins and creating mutations?"

"Besides building an army?" Rain asked. "Probably nothing."

"So if this Prince Fraylee is building an army, and if he has somebody inside with the Templars to help when the time comes, he could basically wipe out everything and be the last thing standing."

"The final battle," Nose Wart agreed.

I was not ready to discuss goblin theology, still, that was sort of what we were looking at when you boiled everything down.

"So the best way to stop this would be to find Prince Fraylee and kill him—" I began to tick off the important points as I saw them, but Rain interrupted.

"We can't kill Prince Fraylee."

"Why not?" Logical question, right?

"He is the last of the males from the royal bloodline. We still need him to pass on his seed."

"Let me get this straight. He has been plotting to wipe you all out, he has been creating an army of mutations, and yet, somebody is still going to be willing to doink this guy just so his bloodline continues?"

"Yes." Rain did not even pause or blink before answering the question.

"Why not name a new family as the royal bloodline and move on? Sheesh, you guys say that I'm stuck in *my* ways!"

"It is not that simple. Prince Fraylee is the last male heir of the original fey Godmother. His blood is old...millennia," Rain whispered with freakish reverence.

"Okay, I'll play along. Let's say we capture this guy alive. What's going to make him agree to pass on anything?"

Other than the fact that he is a guy, and most guys will have sex when they are in the grips of death itself...and not even need foreplay. I mean, seriously, for most guys, foreplay consists of saying, "You wanna?" And then they want to ask if it was "good" for us too? Oh yeah, your hot, feverish body and the smell of vomit on your breath just about put me over the edge. Take me you diseased stallion! Sorry...channeling a bad experience from my human days.

"A female faerie is irresistible to a male faerie if she is experiencing the bleed."

Hmm, that was not going to show up on any Tampax commercials anytime soon, but if that was the case, who was I to say anything? I sure wish that human males were the same. I may be alone here, ladies, but when I used to hit that time of the month, I wanted two things: men and chocolate. That second part was an easy fix. Hell, if I had to return soda bottles for spare change, I could always scrape up enough for a candy bar. However, while there are some guys who don't care, there are more than a few who get all wierded out. After a while, a girl just stops trying. That is probably why you see us tug on the loose sweats and just let ourselves go to hell for a few days. I mean, why should we work hard to tidy up the house if there ain't gonna be any company?

"So you will just have a bunch of women rape this guy until somebody gets knocked up with a boy?"

"Thinking like a hu-man," Nose Wart sing-songed.

"Fine," I huffed. "So we take this guy alive. And we just lock him up until a male heir is spawned. Seems pretty straight forward. I don't think he is going to come peacefully, but we can worry about that when the time comes."

Nose Wart seemed satisfied, and Rain stopped talking, so I just figured we were done until it got dark. I wandered the house. Everybody else had gone on their merry little way. Sure, Supernaturals did not operate in the sunlight, but it only had seriously bad side-effects for some.

I finally went to my room and turned on the television. Nothing helps pass hours like a little quality time with the mind-numbing idiot box. My DVR was packed with all kinds of shows that I guess Lisa had programmed in to record.

I surfed over to VH1 Classic and was totally jazzed to see that it was an 80s rock video block. I quickly remembered my schoolgirl crush on Brian Setzer from The Stray Cats. Him and all those naughty tattoos. Yes, I know that the whole tattoo thing blew up. However, take a peek at *Looks That Kill* by Mötley Crüe. Now watch *Rock This Town* by the Stray Cats. Brian has more than Nikki, Tommy, Vince and Mick combined! Throw in that leather jacket and the motorcycle? Young Ava likey very much, and now? Well, now I just can't believe that I didn't realize how talented Setzer was. He can really beat up that guitar.

So after a few hours of that, it finally started to get dark. Nose Wart knocked on my door.

"Just Ava? Are we ready to go?"

I got up and switched off the television. My mind was made up that, one way or another, I was putting this situation in the "complete" file by the end of the night. And then all I would have left on my list was to find out what the heck Lisa was doing that required her to drug me so she could have Templar meetings in my house.

11

Little Red Corvette

We walked out to the Corvette. I was more than a little surprised to discover a team of hairy, pig-faced little monsters scurrying around my garage with the hood to my precious car up and one of the little freaks actually standing on my engine.

"Greetings, Miss Birch!" they all shouted out together as if somebody had given them a cue.

Their voices had a bit of an animal growl in them that for no reason I can think of immediately reminded me of when Michael Jackson tells that girl to "Go away!" as he turns into a werewolf at the beginning of the *Thriller* video.

Can I beat a dead horse here for just a second? What the heck happened to the "music" part of Music Television? Now, instead of getting Duran Duran, Madonna, Prince, and…(mmm, yummy!) Poison…we get Snooki? Absolutely unfair. In fact, it now seems like every channel out there has simply given up on being what they claim. History Channel? Nope. pawn shop shows, *Ice Road Truckers*, and *Ax Men*. I began my boycott of that channel on Veteran's Day a few years ago when, instead of honoring our troops and the men and women who served by airing specials about World War II, Vietnam, or even the historical stuff like the Revolutionary and Civil Wars, they ran a freakin' *Pawn Stars* marathon!

My granddaddy served in the United States Navy and was at Pearl Harbor when it was attacked. He lost his brother out in that water that morning. I used to sit on his lap and listen to his stories about Pearl and Midway and all of the naval battles he witnessed. He was my hero growing up.

I could go on…like how bidding on people's rented storage spaces or Honey Boo Boos have nothing to teach me, thank you very much TLC. But I think you all get the picture.

"What in the—" I started.

"Miss Birch!" Aoife's voice called from the other end of a pair of long legs that stuck out from under my car. "Please don't be angry. This is my doing."

Aoife pushed herself out from under my car and wiped at her forehead leaving an unbearably perfect little smudge. You know the kind. It was that little dark stain on her face that made her impossibly adorable, whereas on me, it would just look like I needed a shower.

"What is going on here? And…what are these…*things*?" I really did not mean to sound like such a monster snob, but this was my Corvette.

"You have had a few problems with unauthorized entry to your vehicle," Aoife explained. "We are just putting in some added security. Can't have just anybody or anything climbing in to your trunk, now can we, miss?"

I knew she was talking about the trunk of my car, but seriously, you have never met a siren? Everything that comes out of their mouth sounds like sex. No wonder men crashed ships into rocks to try and reach them.

"And you fixed it with the help of these…what are they?" I moved up beside the one who was still standing on top of my precious engine, under the hood like he was in some sort of mysterious cave.

"Oh…you mean the gnolbolds?" Aoife ran a hand down the back ridge of spikes and fur on the closest little beast. It shivered and made what was like a mucousy purr. Yeah…basically nasty.

"No-bolds?" I scratched my head as the word tripped and fell out of my mouth.

"Gnol-bold," Aoife said slowly. "There is a nearly silent 'gu' sound that humans have trouble with."

Sort of like that trilled "R" in Spanish. I never could get my tongue to do it right; at least according to Miss Labredo, my high school Spanish teacher. And did she just call me a 'human'?

"I don't care how you pronounce it. What are these things doing climbing all over my precious Corvette?"

"They won't hurt a thing, miss," Aoife said as she stepped up beside me. "But they have made some modifications that you will appreciate."

"Such as?" I have to admit, I was a bit curious.

"Grug," Aoife called. One of the three-foot tall creatures scurried over, head bowing and bobbing in obvious subservience. "Please break in to the trunk."

I saw a flash of something on the little thing's face for just a moment. It was gone so fast that it could have been my imagination. I watched as Grug scuttled over to the rear of my Corvette. The moment his hands touched the hatch, there was a crackle of blue energy. Grug was shot across the garage and came to a sudden halt as he slammed into the closed garage door. The smell of burnt bacon wafted in the air.

"Holy crap!" I breathed.

I watched the gnolbold slowly stagger to his feet. Smoke rose from his hands and out his ears.

"Umm…"

I was impressed. But I also did not want some innocent person who brushed against my vehicle to get blasted across the parking lot. Well…maybe I did. I hate how people just bang and bump into other people's cars without a care in the world. Those little metal grommets on your jeans leave a nasty scratch if you are not careful.

"Grongle," Aoife called. "Please come and explain the anti-tracking modification."

A reddish-brown gnolbold scampered up and bowed low before me. "If it pleases you, Miss Birch, we removed the tracking device that was located under your front bumper."

Wait...what?

"We have now installed a sensor that will light up an indicator on your dash if another device of this nature is placed. You will have the option of hitting a button that fries the device instantly, or you can choose to leave it. If you leave it, you can allow it to track your actual location, or it will beam a false signal that will make the trackers believe you are someplace else. You can even program in someplace and it will give the impression that you are there."

That all sounded cool, but at the moment I was just a little hung up on the fact that somebody had put a tracking device on my car! Who would bother to even care?

"Would you like to know the source location of the device we located?" the gnolbold asked.

"Absolutely," I growled.

"We have an address for you." The gnolbold handed me a scrap of paper. I looked at the address but it did not ring any bells. It was a local Portland address; that was all.

"And how do I activate this new security system?" I asked as I opened the driver's side door.

"It is automatic. It activates the moment that you stop the car. It is imprinted to you now, so nobody can do anything to your car without you giving permission."

That seemed like a vague and open-ended answer, but I was going to accept it. Maybe that was my first step in leaving behind the ways of my former life as a human. The living Ava would have had a million questions.

I climbed in and turned the key. The engine started and a bunch of stuff flickered and came to life on my windshield. *I am driving the freaking Batmobile*, I thought.

I scanned the display as my two passengers climbed in. Nose Wart curled up on the floor at Rain's feet. If he was okay with that, so was I.

"Greetings, Ava Birch. I am detecting two additional signatures in this vehicle. Do you authorize their occupancy?" a voice said from the speakers. "At least one of these beings is causing you distress. Shall I exterminate?"

"Whoa!" I exclaimed. "No exterminating. Nose Wart is fine. I may not like him, but he serves a purpose. Everybody in the car is fine."

As I backed out of my garage, I made a note to ask what the hell those gnolbolds had done to my car. I had only been kidding when I made that Batmobile reference. Now I was thinking maybe I had KITT from *Knight Rider*.

That Ghoul Ava Kicks Some Faerie A**

12

You Give Love A Bad Name

We hit the road and I let Rain tell me where to go. Turns out that the sidhe location is a lot like my car. It won't just let anybody in. Rain even told me that the physical location that we were driving to at the moment was not where it would be next time. Faeries live in mobile homes. Who knew?

We turned off the main road and down what looked like little more than two dirt tracks through some high grass. We were just outside of the town of Sherwood.

I stopped when Rain told me, and we all climbed out. As soon as I did, the car announced, "Stay safe and return soon, Ava Birch."

Cool!

I followed Rain and Nose Wart into a field with a few horses that looked as if they might be napping. We stopped at a large tree and Rain said something that I doubt my tongue could ever duplicate. If I had trouble with trilling in Spanish, the stuff she was doing would probably end in my choking to death.

A golden glow lit up the tree and then I heard what sounded like a door in *Star Trek* sliding open. Oh come on! Don't pretend you have never seen an episode of *Star Trek*. Geek or not, there are just some things in life that you can't avoid forever.

Rain entered and I followed. The first thing that hit me was this smell that was like cotton candy wrapped in a Cinnabon and dipped in chocolate.

There is so much death here, Adrianna's voice came from what sounded like a distant corridor in my brain.

Okay, that explained the smell. I started forward, but Rain was frozen in her tracks. Nose Wart looked up at her and then at me. He had an expression on his face that I could not even begin to decipher. Goblin facial features are not my forte. Sue me.

"Rain?" I took a step into the long entry hall and touched her arm as I did to see if she might be gently urged into motion. She did not budge one little bit.

"My family…so many dead. I can't go in there," Rain said in a voice barely above a whisper.

"Okay, you wait here," I conceded. "Nose Wart and I will go check things out. Don't move, okay?"

I think she nodded, but I would not swear to it. In any case, I started down the corridor. Nose Wart was right on my heels. If I didn't know better, I would say he was worried that I might leave him behind.

I reached what had to be the main hall. I say that because the room was really long and there were pillars down each side. I am no geologist, but I think they were some sort of green granite. At the far end was an ornate throne. When I say ornate, I am talking enough gold and gemstones to eliminate the national debt. It was in the shape of a small tree whose trunk split to create a sort of seat. All of the branches curved over and formed a canopy of silver leaves.

"The Godmother's throne," Nose Wart breathed in reverence that sounded even stranger coming from the odd little creature.

"Thanks for pointing that out, Captain—" I was about to fire off a sarcastic quip when a new smell drifted into my awareness.

"Alright, vampire, step out where I can see you."

I knew that smell anywhere. Chocolate cake dipped in Dumpster scum.

"It's me, Ava," Jeremy's voice echoed from the darkness.

"If Belinda sent you—" I started, but a voice cut me off.

"I can assure you, Belinda has nothing to do with this." A figure stepped out of a blackness that not even my excellent ghoul vision could penetrate.

He looked like a man. Granted, he looked like a super-hot man except for the nasty sneer on his face. He was holding a very wicked looking blade against Jeremy's throat.

"Prince Fraylee," Nose Wart gasped and dropped face first to the ground.

"And what would a ghoul be doing here in the sidhe?" The prince did not come any closer, but his voice seemed to be right in my ear as if he were standing beside me.

"Just snooping, really," I answered with a shrug as I used my toes on the heels of my shoes to slip out of them.

I was feeling like Billy Jack. And if you don't get that reference, you need to watch the movie. My favorite part was when the bad guy asked Billy Jack how he thought that he might get out of a nasty situation. Billy Jack smiles and says, "I'm gonna take this right foot...and I'm gonna whop you on *that* side of your face (he points to the evil guy's left cheek). And you wanna know something? There isn't a damn thing you're gonna be able to do about it." The he does it! I guess you have to see it to really appreciate it. In any case, I was getting ready for a fight.

"Ava, he's not—" Jeremy began, but was quickly cut off when Prince Fraylee pressed harder with the nasty looking blade.

"Alone?" I tried to sound casual. "Of course he isn't. He probably has a few of his little mutant freaks with him. Maybe, and this is only if I get really lucky, just maybe he has a Templar stashed someplace."

"I have heard a little about you, Miss Birch," Prince Fraylee said with a hint of that typical evil villain chuckle in his voice. "I must say, I expected someone...younger."

Now he was just being a jerk.

"Yeah, well nobody really feels like they are getting what they expected when I show up these days," I said as I brought on the claws—both finger and toe versions.

"Perhaps we can make an arrangement."

I never understand why the bad guy always thinks that he can cut a deal with the (and excuse my presumption, but the series is titled *That Ghoul Ava*) hero. It's like they just assume that the good guy will be driven by the same motivators as they are. If that was the case, Emperor Palapatine would have tucked Luke into his pocket and destroyed the Rebel Alliance, James Bond would be the owner of several small Third World nations and a space station or two, and Shane would be the main character on *The Walking Dead* and The Governor would have lasted less than two episodes.

"Go ahead, I'm listening." Of course those are movie heroes, and don't we always gripe about how stupid they are for passing up on such outlandish offers made by whatever antagonist is currently in their way? Oh...so it's just me? Whatever.

"If you walk away right now, I will give you your own army and more money than you will know what to do with."

Again with the 'give Ava an army' thing. When this was over, I was seriously going to have to do some research on the ghouls of the past. Everybody seems to think that I want or need an army. And that "more money than you know what to do with" line? They obviously have not seen my house or my car.

"How about I make you a deal," I said. And no, it wasn't a question. "You let the cute little vampire go, stop boffing every goblin you can stick your wick in, and then you come back to the faeries and help with the bringing on of a male heir. I guess they think that is a pretty big deal. And if you let me know which Templar has been helping you stir up all of this trouble, I will consider that a personal favor and ask that they not kill you once one of the female faeries gets knocked up with a boy."

"Who are you to make deals with me!" the prince bellowed. "I am Prince Fraylee, sole male heir if the sidhe." He made a big deal about all of that as if maybe he was trying to remind himself. However, he tacked on the next bit with such a casualness, that it was almost humorous and cute. "Oh...and I have a knife to your boyfriend's throat."

"Don't listen to him, Ava!" Jeremy snarled.

The prince gave a flick of his wrist and a thin red line of blood suddenly appeared on Jeremy's throat. I heard a strangled cough and Jeremy flinched. Yeah, I imagine that hurt. I even thought I might have seen a small wisp of smoke come up from the cut. That knife was nasty business.

"Make the deal now, Ava," Prince Fraylee said, almost sounding bored.

"I know how this works," I retorted with a shake of my head. "You get me to agree and then screw me over at the first chance you get."

"Umm…Miss Birch?" I heard a voice from behind me.

"What, Nose Wart?" I didn't dare turn around and give the guy holding the knife a clear shot at my back.

"If he swears the oath here in the sidhe, he is actually bound to it under penalty of death."

"Yeah, and I am sure that he would just give himself over to the proper authorities after he screwed me over." I wasn't born yesterday, you know.

"No, Miss Birch." Nose Wart had actually crawled on his belly to be beside me. "It is not a matter of turning himself in. The sidhe has power."

I looked Prince Fraylee in the eye with the question etched on my face. He simply nodded.

"Yeah, still not good enough," I said with a shake of my head.

"Do you think that I will not end the life of…*this*?" He sort of shook Jeremy. Also, for once, somebody else was being referred to like they were poop on the sole of your best shoes.

I had just a moment to realize that he was manhandling a vampire like it was nothing. What did that say about Prince Fraylee's strength?

"If you are making that human assumption about bluffing, now is a bad time," Nose Wart whispered.

Actually, I hadn't thought of that, but it didn't change much. I realize that you are probably shaking your head in disbelief. "Ava," you might be saying, "he has your boyfriend…he is holding a knife to his throat and threatening to kill him."

You think I don't know that? After all, I am the one standing here. Only, I bet you are the same person who watches a movie or reads a book and yells at the hero when they give in to the bad guy. Seriously, why do people do that? Oh...wait, I know! Because it is a STORY! It makes for more tension or whatever nonsense term they want to label it within literary circles. I was not going to risk the entire Supernatural community for one vampire. I know, not a very good girlfriend.

"To quote the less than popular office of the President of the United States...I don't negotiate with terrorists. So, you either put the knife down, or we escalate this to the point where I have to see what sorts of powers I wield in a fight as a ghoul."

"Fool!" Prince Fraylee spat.

"Sticks and stones."

That was what I was about to say until he cut Jeremy's head off with that knife. There was a moment where I was thinking, *Stupid faerie, you have to run a stake through a vampire's heart.* And then there was a sizzle and Jeremy became a cloud of diamond dust.

Something inside me changed with a click that I felt in my gut. I took a step forward and bared my sharkmouth smile.

"I might just eat you alive for fun...I don't care about male heirs or faerie bloodlines."

Prince Fraylee stuck the knife he had just ended Jeremy with in a sheath at his hip and reached over his shoulder, drawing a non-descript sword.

We were about to get down to business.

13

Fight For Your Right

In the movies and television, a fight scene always has really cool music. One of the most iconic that I can think of is that music in the old *Star Trek* shows: *Duh-duh DA DA DA DA DA duh-duh da da*. For some reason, that is what started playing in my head. I am sure it did nothing for Nose Wart as he watched, but it sure made it a lot more fun for me.

I did a check of the hall to see what sorts of places things might be able to jump out from. I knew that no human could sneak up on me, but I was not willing to risk that I could sense another Supernatural.

The room was probably two hundred yards long and about fifty yards wide. Basically it was freaking huge. The pillars were set at about twenty foot intervals and split the room into neat thirds.

The prince moved closer, the look on his face was absolute calm. He looked like he did this kind of thing every day. As for me, I was finding this strange sense of tranquility in my *Star Trek* music. I was trying my best to recall anything from a show that I could copy or try to imitate in battle. Did I forget to mention the fact that I was never much of a fighter?

121

After what seemed like way too long, the two of us were finally within striking distance. A flash of inspiration came and I let it flow. I brought my right hand up beside my face and gave my fingers a little wiggle in what I was hoping mimicked Freddy Krueger.

"Last chance," I said in a voice that sounded way tougher than I felt at that moment.

Prince Fraylee just stood there with his hands clutching the hilt of his sword. His gaze never left mine. And that is why I finally saw something that was just a little surprising. It was like my focus shifted to Bionic Woman mode and zoomed in on the slight creases at the corners of his astonishingly purple eyes. He was nervous! Or at least that was what I was telling myself.

Of course, a second later he took a big swing with that sword and it was time to fight. I jumped back and avoided the first swing with an ease that had me just about ready to think that this was easy...until the backswing came. A half second's worth of reaction is what kept my head still attached to my neck. I would marvel at my own speed later, but for the time being, I needed to pay attention.

He jabbed with the point, but that was just to get me to back up. After the third such poke, I figured he was trying to get me to move someplace specific. Good for me! I ducked as a hairy paw came out of a shadows.

I tucked and rolled to the left and came up with the first of my own attacks. My left hand barely slowed as I cut through the thick brown fur of a bugbear. The creature howled and tried to keep his insides from falling out; he was now far too busy to be a threat to me any longer.

I danced away at another slash from the prince, but he managed to nick my left arm just below the shoulder. I actually heard the hiss a second before a fiery pain shot up and down the entire length of my arm. My wince and reaction gave him an opening, and he came in with a whirling move that would have been pretty to watch if it was not trying to cut me in half.

On instinct, I threw up my hand to hopefully protect myself. That is not a defense that I recommend...unless you have razor sharp claws that are apparently unbreakable. Seriously, if I could get the formula of whatever my nails are made of and bottle it for women, we could put the press-on nail business in the ground.

There was a nasty screeching sound that was only mildly annoying for me, but the prince actually staggered back and went to cover his ears. Now it was my turn to exploit an opening.

I have no idea if it is just something that comes naturally to ghouls, but I began to slash with my hands and even threw a few wheel-kicks in for good measure to keep him off balance. I was pulling some serious *Crouching Tiger, Hidden Dragon* stuff. If I would have thought about it, I might have even added in a few Bruce Lee 'HEE-yaws' instead of the snarls and heavy breathing. Again, if it were not for the fight music from *Star Trek* going on in my head, this would have almost been boring.

I had gotten in to some kind of rhythm...which is why I did not see a piece of the wall detach and start my way. I will never admit it to his face, but Nose Wart saved my little gray butt at that moment.

"Have care behind you, miss!" a voice waded through the repetitious theme song playing on my mental loop.

I glanced just in time to catch the equivalent of a bowling ball-sized rock up side my head. I went flying in a spectacular but graceless fashion and only stopped when my body collided with one of those granite pillars.

Yep...I said ouch, too.

I was only to my knees when the rock troll arrived, looming above me with its giant boulder fists. Yeah, I said 'it'. You try to distinguish between the sexes of a rock troll when it is trying to smash you into pulp.

My only defense at that moment was to roll sideways. I heard the crunching boom echo through the hall as stone met stone. I had no idea that rocks could actually spark.

On hands and knees I scrambled, but had to hurriedly toss myself to the side again as Prince Fraylee seemed to appear from out of nowhere with his sword moving faster than a blender blade on margarita night.

I had the back of the rock troll...or so I thought until I was midair and flying with hands and feet extended to hopefully plunge all twenty of my switchnails into it. The head turned like Linda Blair's in *The Exorcist* and it made a noise that I was almost sure was a laugh. That backhand reversed my direction in an instant. I thought I heard something crack in my chest, but I simply switched from *Star Trek* to the Indian Jones theme and increased the volume in my head.

DA da-duh-duh...da-duh-duh...DA da-duh-duh, da-duh-duh DUH DUH.

I landed on my back and rolled heels-over-head, coming to a stop and actually springing to my feet where I was able to step just to the left and bring my right hand in a rake down the side of the rock troll. A big appendage fell to the ground and what I was almost positive had to be magma began to ooze like blood from where the arm used to be. The huge creature made a sound that reminded me of a pepper grinder being broadcast through speakers at a Van Halen concert.

In a flash, I came in low and drove my left hand into its back...or front. With its head able to turn in a three-sixty, it was impossible to tell. I intended to shed its heart; I never intended to pull it out of the thing's chest. Honest!

In my hand was the biggest diamond that I had ever seen. A bit of magma dripped off of it, but a girl knows a diamond when she sees it. I quickly got a fix on Prince Fraylee who was staring in disbelief as another of his unnatural spawn had met its end at my claws. That gave me a second to very carefully put the softball-sized precious stone on the floor with a gentle reverence.

"Nose Wart?" I called.

"Yes, miss?"

"You see that big stone I just set down?"

"Yes, miss."

"Guard it with your life until I finish with the prince?"

"Yes, miss."

And that was all the time I had as Prince Fraylee came at me in another flurry of swipes, jabs, and slashes. I kept telling myself that I needed to go on the attack, but he was not giving me the chance. It took all that I had to bat away blow after blow. And I was not exactly a hundred percent successful.

I took a few nasty cuts here and there. Each one made a loud hiss like when you put the pan you just finished cooking bacon with in the kitchen sink and turn on the water. Yeah, I know grease and water are a bad mix. Maybe I will share that story with you at another time.

At last, the prince backed away for a second. He glared at me with absolute hatred that I did not think I was deserving of until I remembered that I had killed two of his "children" right before his eyes. I imagine that would piss most people off.

"I will feed your broken body to a dragon and then burn the dung in a furnace," Prince Fraylee said in a whisper.

"A flare for the over dramatic...wait! Did you just say you would feed me to a dragon?"

There is no way that dragons can be real and nobody know anything about it! Seriously, people report Bigfoot, poor Nessie over in Scotland can't come up for a few rays of sun without people having a conniption fit...and don't even get me started on UFOs. Now this guy throws out dragons like it is perfectly normal.

Still, I was glad that he had finally seen fit to give me a chance to catch my breath. I glanced down at my body and was just a little annoyed at the several cuts and slices I had apparently taken. My top was little more than a bunch of rags. And when I say top...I am seriously minimizing it...this was one of my vintage Cinderella concert tees from when I saw them on the Gypsy Road tour. Sure, I could probably replace it on eBay, but that was not the same. I bought this one at the actual event!

"You are gonna pay for this, you little faerie bastard!" I growled.

This time, it was me that went on the attack. Now Prince Fraylee fell back while doing his best to parry and dodge my attacks. Have you ever watched a fight scene and wondered what the characters were thinking? Well, for me, besides having the Indiana Jones theme blaring, I was also hearing Daffy Duck.

"HO! Ha-ha...guard, turn, parry, dodge, spin, HA, thrust!"

I felt my claws meet resistance once when I came in low. Five evenly spaced lines showed up on his thigh. Bright red blood that seemed to almost glow began to ooze from the injury. Even better was the look of surprise on old princey-poo's face. He was not good at blocking out the pain.

"Come, my children!" he yelled as my assault continued with a flurry.

I felt the floor begin to vibrate and a low rumble that was almost at a subconscious level made my teeth buzz. And then I smelt something...hot. That was the only thing I could equate it to. Not spicy, no...I am talking about blazing desert sun. I know. Not a very helpful description, but that was what came to mind.

And then they stepped out from some corridor behind the throne. Never in my life had I imagined anything like them.

Well over ten feet tall, I bet the NBA would love these guys. Their orange skin was covered in what looked like warts and they had wild red hair and even crazier beards despite the fact that one of them was obviously female. They wore what looked like sewn together lizard skins that barely covered their naughty parts. His looked like a scaly jock strap and she was wearing a bikini type thing that would embarrass a porn star.

"Fiery jötnar!" Nose Wart shrieked.

"Yote-nar? Can't you just call them giants or something simple?" I took a step back and the prince took that opportunity to scurry away and catch his breath.

"Kill the ghoul," Prince Fraylee heaved. Hmm, so much for making me suffer and feeding me to dragons.

And then they charged. I crouched and waited until they were almost right on top of me before I jumped with all I had, hoping that my leaping ability would get me over. Note to self: dial it back just a little. I clipped my head on the vaulted ceiling almost sixty feet above. By the time I landed, the two big oafs were skidding to a stop. I darted in and slashed low at the back of the legs of the one on the left which turned out to be the female. She roared and stumbled. Unfortunately, the male had a clear shot and took it. He punted me the length of the hall. I hit the back wall and heard something wet upon impact. That couldn't be good.

Things sort of got fuzzy around the edges. I tried to stand, but my legs were not listening. This was definitely bad.

Stop that infernal song long enough to take a big sniff, you idiot! a voice from somewhere down a long hallway in my brain yelled.

I did, but the rush of pain made me practically seize up into a ball. However, as I lay there in the fetal position cursing Adrianna for tricking me into letting down my guard, the smell of something yummy hit me. My eyes tracked over to where the bugbear sat against the wall, eyes glazed in death, insides in a heap in its lap.

Supper time!

I scrambled over, my eyes tracking the fiery jötunn as he struggled with his desire to either help what I now assumed was either his mate or his sister...or...eww...both; or come pound me into a stain on the stone floor.

"Leave her, you imbecile!" Prince Fraylee was screaming. "Finish that bitch while she is down!"

That was not very nice at all. And fortunately, it seemed that blood (or love) was thicker than water. The jötunn ignored the command and knelt by his fallen female. My guess was that I had completely severed the Achilles tendon. I don't care who you are, that has to sting.

I took the time to scoop the easily available innards into my gaping mouth in a single bite. Mmm...sweeter than candy!

Oh don't get all heebie jeebie. You do remember that I am a ghoul. Yes, I realize I normally spare you the details, but with the situation being what it was, I did not have time to down the entire body; I had to take what was made easily available.

I felt things inside me physically start to shift. As I eyed the rest of my potential meal with longing, the male fiery jötunn, or whatever the heck it was, rose and gave me a look of what I had to assume to be hatred. His woman was hurt and it was my fault.

Rage and anger make a person sloppy. Remember that the next time that you are in a pickle.

The mountain of a beast came at an all-out run. That made it far too easy to dodge at the last second. And that was when I gave him an injury to match his girlfriend's. My claws raked the back of his legs and I even heard what sounded like a giant rubber band being snapped. He stumbled and landed with a meaty crash, howling in such a way that hurt my ears. It echoed off the walls and seemed to fill the room with a physical presence.

I didn't have time to revel in my victory. I heard the click-clack of the prince's boots as he strode for me in a big hurry. Something told me that this was not going to end well. I guess I would make my apologies to the faeries later, because this would now most likely be to the death.

I was able to get to my feet and turn before he reached me. However, his sword was not up in the attack position. Oh...and he was not looking at me. I followed his gaze to the male jötunn. He had that look that only a parent can have when one of their children is hurt.

He was speaking, but it was in a language that I could not begin to guess. It didn't sound like anything that I had ever heard before. When he turned back to me, I saw traces of silver running down his cheeks.

"My children...what have you done to my children?"

Yep, he sounded like most every parent I had ever met. Did you hear the one about a bunch of kids in some rich neighborhood that broke into one of the houses while the owner was on vacation? So they have this drunken festival and post the pictures on Twitter. You can see them spray-painting his walls, urinating on his floors, breaking windows, and destroying his furniture; so basically doing what over privileged teens call "fun". The owner finds out exactly who when he is told by his own teen.

Instead of having the little delinquents hauled in, he posts the pictures on a web site and asked them to come forward and make right the damage; you know...help clean it up and maybe pitch in to cover the costs. The parents of some of these little monsters...no, I take that back, I have met actual monsters, and these kids are far worse. These parents are threatening to sue the homeowner, saying things like how this might hurt their kids' chances of getting in to a good college. Seriously?

So now I have the prototypical bad parent standing here asking me how I could dare hurt his children. The same ones that were, just moments before, trying to smash me into ghoul jelly.

"I gave you the chance to come peacefully," I said as I climbed to my feet.

I felt a bit woozy and edged closer to the dead bugbear. Strange how he was so worked up over the jötnar, but had not seemed the least bit bothered that I had ripped the heart out of his troll and disemboweled his bugbear. I guess parents have their favorites.

"It is time for the fey to stop hiding. Maybe it is time that the insect known as human have some of its homes leveled...destroyed." The prince was glaring at me like I was the one taking a bulldozer to the rain forest.

"So you wipe out a bunch of your own. How is that supposed to motivate anybody to help?"

"It will serve as a message to the other sidhe. Either come and join in the fight, or be considered one of the enemy."

I never get that approach. Join or die. Seriously, how do crazy dictators pull it off? Of course, if he had these giants delivering the ultimatum, I bet it would be hard to refuse.

"Well that ship has sailed. And you still have a chance to come out of this alive. Tell me who you are working with in the Templars...and while you are at it, why would also help."

"Isn't it obvious?" Prince Fraylee asked with a tone that I was becoming terribly accustomed to hearing when I dealt with other Supernaturals.

"Honestly?" I shrugged my shoulder. "No, it is not even a little bit obvious to me. And nobody I know has tossed out any good reason either. The Templars are supposed to be like the police of the Supernatural world."

"Is that what they told you?" The prince laughed with genuine amusement. "Silly ghoul, the Templars were created to eliminate *you*. The truce came when they suffered grievous losses after failing at their first assignment."

"Wiping out the ghouls was their first assignment?"

I had only heard a very small part of the Templar story up until now, but I did not think what the prince was saying had any real truth to it. The Templars were not created to wipe out ghouls. From what little I knew, they were just a version of the police of the Supernatural community.

I was going to have to do some reading when this was over. Oh well, with *Breaking Bad* gone, there wasn't all that much on television that interested me lately except for *The Big Bang Theory*. That Amy…she always makes me smile.

"In the war against the unholy…yes," the prince spoke in what I felt was a bit of an overly self-righteous tone. Funny thing about nut jobs and lunatics…they are always so busy seeing what is wrong with everybody else that they often miss the fact that they are nuttier than grandma's fruitcake.

"Hold on. Who are you calling unholy. I was a good Catholic girl."

Okay, that was only partially true. I went to Catholic school during seventh and eighth grade. And maybe I dressed like one for fun a couple of times. Still, I was not unholy. I touched crosses…in fact I still wear one. I went in to a church and scooped up some holy water when I had to deal with some vamps.

"You are an abomination," the prince replied. He did not say it with any nastiness or anything. He simply stated it as a fact. Like he would say I was female. There was no emphasis on the word "abomination" or any sort of indication that he was saying it in a derogatory fashion.

"But you're not?" I figured that, if he was part of the Supernatural world, then he must fall in to the same category.

"I am not undead." When he said that, he actually laughed. "Has your Psychic taught you nothing?"

Apparently not.

"You seem to want to place everything in one category. There are creatures like faeires, nymphs, goblins and sylphs that are accepted as normal. And then there are those that are considered unnatural. Ghouls, vampires, ghosts and such. The

130

Templars believe that nothing should be allowed back across the veil of death."

Monster racism…great.

"Still, that does not really justify your coming in and wiping out an entire community of faeries. You killed your own friends and family."

"If I was not willing to put them to death, how would any of the other fey take my threat seriously?"

Again with the extreme logic. Can't just kill one or two. Nope, gotta waste everybody. Just plain stupid if you ask me.

"But what do the Templar get from all of this?" Maybe a different line of questioning would shed some light on things.

"They are human, they get what humans always crave. Money…power…a sense of dominion."

"But you would be starting an extinction event that would affect every Supernatural."

"Actually, I have assurances that it would just be the unholy. The undead like vampires, banshee…*ghouls*."

The prince turned his back on me and knelt beside the downed giant that was whimpering like a big baby. While he was busy, I took the chance to lop off the legs of the bugbear with my toeblades. I got one down before he returned his attention to me.

"I hope you enjoy your last meal," he snarled, anger renewed and sword back up to fighting position.

"Not bad," I said with a shrug as I felt something happening to my left arm. I had not even noticed how it was sporting an extra joint between the elbow and the wrist. That section of my arm straightened out as if some invisible force were pulling it.

I took a step back to allow whatever hocus pocus was going on with my arm to finish. By the time the prince reached me, I was as ready as I could be. *Hungry Like The Wolf* was playing in my head. Didn't feel like fight music, but I wasn't going to pick now to argue with my mental DJ.

The next several seconds were pretty boring. We circled left, circled right, jabbed, but nothing really happened.

"Just kill her already!" a female voice called as a familiar figure stepped out of the shadows.

14

Wanted: Dead or Alive

"Why am I not surprised?" I tried to say with as little emotion as possible.

"I told you that you were messing with things of which you had no idea," Merriette said as she strolled out casually from an unnatural darkness in one corner. I wondered how long she had been watching.

"So who got fed to the lake troll?" I asked, shifting just enough so that both faeries were in front of me.

"Godiva served her new Godmother as was her destiny," Merriette spoke as she moved with Jessica Rabbit-like sultriness.

"And so you were in on this little scheme from the start?" Obvious question, but I was really just stalling for time. The sword on her hip was not going unnoticed, and up until now, I had been doing my best at keeping the prince from slicing me up.

"The fey have stayed silent for too long," Merriette announced as she drew the blade from its scabbard. "We have been forbidden from going out in public because the humans are so weak and find us irresistible. We are punished for our beauty while unholy creatures, such as yourself, are allowed to walk

133

about freely. But if that were not bad enough, the humans continue to destroy our homes, forcing us time and again to relocate."

It wasn't that I did not see her point. Well, all except for the "unholy" bit; I would argue that until I was blue...err...hmm...flesh tone? Yeah, flesh tone in the face.

"We will do away with your kind, and then, with a little help, we will assume control of the Templars and bring the entire Supernatural world to heel!" Prince Fraylee said with glee usually reserved for children who just got told that they are going on a family vacation to see Mickey and Minnie.

What is it with me and individuals who get a *Pinky and the Brain* complex...heavy on the Brain. I can barely manage my own life, much less get all "rule the world" on folks.

"You realize that these things never end well...and who would want to rule the entire world anyways? Think of all the paperwork!" Yep, still stalling. That sword she held looked sort of sharp.

Don't knock it 'til you try it, Adrianna's voice piped up in my head.

And look where that got you? I snapped, careful to keep my inner dialog inside where it belonged.

Yes, but I would have gotten away with it if— she started, but I cut her off.

If it weren't for you meddling kids, I quipped in my best unmasked-evil-old-man villain at the end of the *Scooby Doo* episode voice.

I sensed her confusion and only had a brief moment to pity her. The faeries were on the move and fanning out to make this really hard on me.

"And you trust the Templars to not take you out as soon as all the dirty work is done?" Back to stall tactics. I did not like the way Merriette was swishing that long, thin blade of hers around. It was a blur and she did not look like she was even trying.

"Of course not," Merriette scoffed. "That is why we have been slowly building an army of our own."

"The mutants." I had not meant to say that out loud, and

Adrianna repeated those same words in unison with mine. But then she had more to add on the subject.

That is genius, the Templars won't be able to develop weapons fast enough to deal with the variations. It will be a slaughter, I think I actually felt Adrianna bouncing with evil glee.

"But what about this supposed evil Templar land developer guy...ruined forests...all that garbage you heaped on me that night in the mall?"

"All true," Merriette shrugged. "Only, it was me who told them exactly where to cut and burn this time, it was me who brought my brother and the kill squads in and provided a distraction so that they could do what needed to be done. I gave them a list of who to spare and let them do what they wished with the rest."

"Do what they wished?" That did not sound good.

"Humans are so predictable. A few of them have been waiting for their chance to take a faerie female as their own. So, some were killed, some were spared for my new sidhe where I will rule as Godmother, and some were...offered."

"But why get involved with the Templars? And why all that nonsense at the mall?"

"Silly ghoul," Merriette laughed in a way that was sickeningly pleasant, but full of evil, "do you know nothing of your heritage?"

"Not really," I admitted with a shrug.

"Well I don't have time for a history lesson, but in the simplest terms, it was a ghoul who killed Aphrodite...the first Godmother. Ever since then, we have tried without success to rid the world of your kind. It has taken us this long to finally get one of our own in with the Templars, and now they will finish the job that they should have completed centuries ago. But why stop with ghouls? It is time that we resume our place as gods among men like it was in the days of old." She and the prince both shared a look and laughed in that stereotypical evil villain way.

"And as for that night in the mall?" Merriette was starting to warm up her sword arm with little slashes back and forth. "Nothing more than an entertaining distraction. Besides, we needed a way to flush you out. I was surprised it worked so quickly and easily, to be honest. To think that a ghoul was right here in our own back yard, as the humans like to say. When we heard that the Godmother had spotted one of your kind in public, I knew it was time to put our plan into motion."

It took me a second, but then I recalled that little incident at the pizza place in Estacada. Funny how something so random could trigger such an odd series of events. However, I would not have time to give that much thought at the moment; apparently the conversation was over.

Merriette and Prince Fraylee rushed in to attack. I took a few steps back and vaulted over their heads, landing just behind the pair as they were skidding to a halt. Merriette was the first to spin and deftly deflected my claws with her blade, but I landed a nice shot on Fraylee who, to his credit, bit back anything beyond a slight wince and hiss.

I jumped again, this time back and away from them to open up some space. In my head, I heard that familiar guitar jangling as the still dreamy Jon Bon Jovi crooned about being wanted...dead or alive. It didn't really have anything to do with my situation, but I was also very aware that the final outcome would be decided right here.

There would be no limping away to lick the wounds for a second and even more exciting confrontation. And you can probably tell by the number of pages left in this book that the story is wrapping up here pretty quick.

This would be it. I would kill them or they would kill me. As strange as it may seem, I felt okay with that little nugget of knowledge in my brain. Honestly, I was a bit tired of this adventure.

Merriette came in from my left, and I think she expected the prince to be there with her. He was being more cautious after having felt what my claws could do. Still, she was fearless; probably from decades or centuries of practice hefting a blade. She came high, but I noticed that her eyes flashed to my middle. On instinct, I threw a downward slashing block with my right hand and her sword rang like a bell as it showered us both with blue and green sparks. My left hand shot out and I felt a slight hesitation before the claws sunk deep into her chest.

Her eyes went wide with a mix of fear, shock, and intense agony. Blood spewed from her lips in a sapphire blue mist. I jerked my hand up and over, shredding her insides.

"Take the head, miss!" a hoarse voice yelled.

My right hand came back like I was John McEnroe returning a lob from Bjorn Borg. And if you have no idea what I'm talking about…it was back when tennis was actually fun to watch. Yeah…I know.

Merriette was still staring at me despite the fact that her head was now a good three feet from her body. A fountain of blood and then, as best I can describe it, an implosion. The body seemed to collapse on itself in the blink of an eye. The tinkle of tiny pebbles hitting the floor could be heard through the bluish cloud of faerie dust.

I had no time to marvel or even admire the moment. Prince Fraylee shrieked like a girl and came at me again. Remember that little thing I mentioned back when I was being charged by a ten foot tall giant about rage making you careless? Well, this would be another example.

There was no switch to the hacking attempts that the prince was making. For all his finesse, he might as well be trying to chop wood. I didn't even have to work all that hard. It was simply a matter of holding my hand up and swatting his attacks to the left or right.

His face had a glowing sheen to it and silvery tracks were visible on both cheeks from his tears. Again and again he chopped. At last, he started to falter. And then the moment that I was waiting for finally came.

Prince Fraylee reared back, but at the top of his swing, he had to pause to suck in some much needed oxygen. When he did, I came in under his arms with both sets of finger blades. All ten plunged in from either side and I actually felt them scrape one another as they met in the middle.

The prince just stood there…staring at me. The sword came

free from his loosened grip and clattered to the floor. I didn't really hear it over the Ritchie Sambora guitar solo in my head, but I saw his mouth opening and closing like a landed fish.

Without things like fuzzy edges and slow motion, these scenes are just not nearly as cool. The rest of the scene played out pretty much like the previous one. I took his head and he turned into a blue cloud of faerie dust.

I slumped to the floor thinking that I could lose the mental soundtrack, but as soon as I did, the pain came like nobody's business. It was the sort of pain that makes a person vomit. I started to slip into Ava's Magic Playland as I saw Nose Wart scampering for me. Bless his heart, he was carrying a bugbear leg.

I made short work of the furry beast's remains and horked up a hairball for my trouble. Unfortunately, that was the only thing close that was currently edible. The troll had turned to a pile of stones and I doubted that it would help me at all if I ate them. Oh…and they had no discernible smell.

The two giants were huddled close and unfortunately still very much alive. Of course, it would be next to nothing for me to remedy their…condition. And I admit it was crossing my mind to the point where I was struggling to my feet.

Ava HUNGRY!

Something struck me in the side and I paused in mid-stride as I was about to satisfy some serious cravings. I could smell them as they still struggled to staunch the bleeding from my earlier slices. Mmm-mmm…barbecue!

"Ava!" a voice barked.

I recognized it and spun. My stomach churned in a way that an entire bottle of Prilosec would not quell. Vampires are so gross!

Belinda was a safe distance away, not that I would eat her. But at that moment, I'm not sure that she was confident with that possibility. She was holding the body of an obscenely obese man with one hand at her side like it was a piece of luggage.

The smell was divine! Fresh corpses are like fresh baked bread to a ghoul. It has a smell all of its own that seems to sink into your pores.

She tossed the body with no real effort and it landed about two feet in front of me. I looked down at the body and was only briefly aware that the throat had been ripped out in a rather nasty fashion.

I have some experience with vampires now, or at least enough to know that they are notoriously clean eaters. This was not a vampire feeding; it was murder.

Wow, I absolutely don't care in the slightest! Food, glorious food, like the little orphans sing in *Oliver!* I went to work making the body go away while Belinda was saying something about "a three time loser" and how "prison was too good for guys like him" while also making disparaging remarks about my eating habits. I didn't care…this chubby little man was reaching all the right spots for me. I was almost done when something that Belinda said caused me to pause.

"I would have never believed it if not for seeing it with my own eyes. I mean, I have heard…everybody has heard about the ability of the ghoul to overcome certain…obstacles. But you are absolutely the most frightful thing that I believe I have ever beheld…and considering that I spent many of my nights creeping through battlefields and feeding on those left behind by Vandals, Visigoths, Carthaginians, and Romans…not to mention those glorious Norsemen…"

True to form, Belinda was carrying on with her monolog, but I had stopped eating. I still had part of fat boy's leg jutting from one side of my mouth like a stogie. I had no idea what she was talking about. I rose to my feet, being very careful to continue to let my mind wander wherever it chose. At the moment, I was seeing the dance sequence from *The Breakfast Club*. Who would have believed that geeky little Anthony Michael Hall would grow up to be such a hunk? Seriously, if you never saw that little USA series, *The Dead Zone*, you are probably having a very hard time picturing him as anything other than the stereotypical geek from the great films of John Hughes.

Of course I did not have so much as a compact with a mirror on me, but I was suddenly very curious. I looked around until I spotted Nose Wart. He was busy picking up all of the sapphires that had spilled on the floor. Also, I noticed a whisk broom and a few small bags near the piles of faerie dust.

"Nose Wart, do you know where a mirror might be found?" I hadn't really ventured around inside the sidhe, but I had to guess that there were living quarters. I should be able to find at least one mirror.

"Yes, miss...follow me, miss," Nose Wart chirped and scampered away past the throne.

I shot a withering look at the two huddling giants as I passed when it looked like they were about to stand up. As hungry as I still was, they did not want to piss me off. To their credit, they both resumed clutching one another and making low rumbling whispers of what I had to guess were words of comfort by the tone.

I reached the hallway where Nose Wart waited, hopping back and forth from one foot to another. Something had him in a tizzy.

"Do you have to use the bathroom?" I asked as I elbowed past and opened the first door.

I felt something like a teensy electric shock sort of ripple across my skin. Brushing it aside, I stepped in to a room that would embarrass a New York City penthouse dweller. To say lush or extravagant would be a huge understatement.

Looking around the room, I saw hallways leading off in several directions. The place was beyond huge. But, I was standing in the doorway. I had not gone so far that I could not lean my head back and look into the hallway. Yep, just as I'd thought, there was another door less than five feet from this one. However, if I leaned back into the room, there was no door just to my right as there should be.

Oh well, I could not be bothered with that right now. I was on a quest, but where had Nose Wart gone? I stepped back out into the hallway and he had retreated all the way to the entrance chamber. He was busy slapping at himself and I saw tendrils of smoke rising from several patches.

"Are you coming?" I asked.

He shook his head emphatically from side to side in a very definite negative. He was looking at me with wide, frightened eyes.

"You are on fire, miss," he managed to finally say.

I looked down and, sure enough, light blue flames like a natural gas stove pilot light were flickering all over my skin. Well that could not be good.

"Wards," the goblin whispered in obvious fear.

I tried patting them out, but oddly enough, they would kick right back up. I walked back out to the hall and found that they stayed out once extinguished. I didn't know what a ward was, but I was smart enough to figure out that some sort of magic was keeping me out of that room.

"*Stahd*," a gravel-filled voice said from behind me. I turned to see the male jötunn had crawled over on his belly.

He nodded and then pointed down the hall. I took a step and then another. No shock…not even a tingle. I gave myself a brief inspection and was pleased to see no signs of fire.

I walked back into that first apartment, or whatever faeries called these rooms. After a few minutes, I discovered a bedroom with a golden four-post bed. I resisted the urge to fall into it and sleep for about a week and instead walked over to the far wall…that was entirely paneled in floor-to-ceiling mirrors.

To be honest, I did not recognize that it was me I was seeing for a few seconds. The image that stared back at me with jet black orbs was a hideous monster. And it was not simply that I was in full Sharkmouth, or that my fingers and toes were all sporting several inches of extra sharp nailage.

I had to tilt my head to one side and then the other to confirm that what I was seeing was actually me! There were slices all over my body. What little of my clothing that remained was only clinging to me, adhered by the thick, black, syrupy blood that was still oozing from a few of the nastier wounds.

Funny, but during the fight, I was certain that I had deflected every attack. Or at least most of them. Looking at the reflection in the mirror, I had to wonder if I had managed to deflect a single one.

My mind had done something else on its own…it went to the only thing that could keep me from feeling what had been done. There was Brett Michaels in his prime…cavorting on stage with C.C DeVille and Bobby Dall with the not even slightly cute in a weird way Rikki Rockett banging on his drums to *Nothin' But A Good Time*.

Funny thing about that album, *Open Up And Say Ahhh…*, the cover was eventually censored. When it first came out, there was this naughty girl painted like a tiger with a tongue sticking out that would make Gene Simmons say "Damn!" Of course Tipper Gore and her evil minions were busy getting ratings put on records and screaming that everything was indecent or immoral. The album (back when albums existed) was re-released with an all black cover and a stripe where all you could see were the girl's eyes. Sort of a reverse dirty movie stripe.

"Ava!" a voice snapped me back. It was Rain. When had she gotten here, and why was the female giant with her? And was that Belinda?

My gaze returned to the image in the mirror and my concentration finally slipped. I think I screamed. I know I fainted.

15

Poison Arrow

"Ava?" the voice was coming from someplace close. I knew that voice…it was a good voice. Friend.

Something cold slipped past my lips. Yummy. I opened my mouth, hoping that whatever invisible source that was feeding me would continue.

"You can open your eyes, Ava," that voice said.

I didn't really want to. The last time they had been open, I had seen something horrible, only to realize that it was me. It was worse than that time my friend had convinced me that despite having dropped out after only two weeks, she knew all she needed to do my hair. I had asked for the Jennifer Aniston cut and style, but what I got was more like the Peggy Bundy.

"If you don't open your eyes, no more food. I have a freshly dead wino here that is gonna go to waste."

"Are there any mirrors in here?" I asked meekly.

"In your basement? Why would there be mirrors down here?" Lisa asked with a snort.

"I'm…I'm home?"

"You've been home for almost three weeks."

"Huh?"

143

That seemed like a long time, but for me it had only been a few seconds. It all came back in a rush; the battle, killing Prince Fraylee and Merriette. And Belinda had been there…

"We got the word that you put down the prince, and that Merriette was dead as well. That did not sit to keenly with the few survivors of the sidhe. You basically eliminated the oldest bloodline in fey history," Lisa said.

I opened my eyes and took in the comforting and familiar sights of my basement. I also noticed that Lisa had taken the time to dismember the body that I had eaten all but the torso of up to this point. Somebody was getting over her squeamishness.

Sitting up, I was a little surprised to discover a familiar goblin curled up in a corner like a twisted parody of a pet cat. I was a lot surprised when I saw a few dozen more goblins in little piles of three or four scattered around the room. But it did not stop there…oh no. A bugbear was busy sweeping and three more were in bunk beds!

"What the…" my voice trailed off.

"Yeah, I was just about to get to that part," Lisa said with a sigh. "We have some company. I think we are going to need a bigger house…someplace away from the city most likely."

She went on to explain that there were close to a hundred assorted creatures that the prince had sired. Most would stay with the faeries, but a few had asked to be placed in my service. Rain and Morgan had hammered out the details. Oh, and Rain was the new Godmother.

I asked her how Belinda had ended up there and was told that that she had felt Jeremy's death. Vampires have some sort of mental link between them that is shared by members of a Kiss and she was able to see the last minutes of his life through his eyes. If that was the case, then she had seen that I let him die in a manner of speaking. I only briefly wondered if that was going to come back and bite me in the ass.

I guess Belinda was there in a flash, but Rain would not let her inside. Faeries and vampires don't get along very well…long story, and Sookie tells it better. She told Belinda that she would only let her in if she brought me something to eat. Apparently

Rain had peeked in a few times and watched as the battle raged. She knew that I would need to heal. Also, I imagine she was not too fond of the idea of having a ghoul slip into *Famé Rabbia* in the sidhe. That would explain the dead body Belinda tossed me, although how she acquired it is a story all of its own and will probably serve me later when I need to distract myself…lucky you!

Just then, the door to my once peaceful basement sanctuary now turned mutant flop house banged open. Literally stomping down the stairs (and yes, I do actually mean literally) was Aoife. She was scowling and her fists were clenched tight enough to have turned her hands an even whiter shade of white that verged on glowing.

"I will put them all on ships and crush them between Scylla and Charybdis!" she huffed.

Wasn't that something from a song by The Police? Oh well, I could look it up later.

"What now?" Lisa turned to address the siren before I could open my mouth. Somebody had slipped into the role of den mother quite easily in my…absence.

"Those bloody jötnar!" she snapped as if that was enough of an answer.

"Wait!" I climbed to my feet and was rewarded with the room doing a rather acrobatic tilt to the left and then the right as if it were trying to knock me off my feet. "The giant thingies are here? Where in the hell did you put them?"

"The garage," Lisa answered over her shoulder as she started to follow Aoife up the stairs to put an end to whatever problem was currently manifesting itself.

It only took me a few seconds for my brain to remind me that was where my beautiful Corvette should be parked. I did not see how it would be possible for them to be sharing that space with my car and not end up scratching and denting it every time they moved.

I headed up the steps and felt something practically adhere to my left hip. I looked down to see Nose Wart looking up at me with his rheumy eyes and raggedy teeth that were in serious need of some floss.

"Please don't kill us and eat us, miss!" he pleaded.

Where that was coming from, I had no idea. I don't think I had ever given any indication that he or his fellow goblins were on my menu…had I? I shrugged and resumed my trek up the stairs.

A slight whimper followed me up. I stopped and turned to face the little beast. Have you ever seen those "Ugliest Dog" contests? Well I suddenly realized what Nose Wart reminded me of. There are those ugly, practically hairless, but with enough well-placed tufts in random places to look horrible, little dogs that have the warts and moles all over their mottled skin. Well if you trained one to walk upright and gave it a more piggish snout? That would be a goblin. How could I eat him now? Crap…I had a pet.

"I won't eat you as long as you don't give me a reason." I decided to keep it open ended; never know what the future might hold.

As I stepped into my kitchen, I was more than a little surprised to discover Betty and Morgan at my table sipping something from mugs. They both did a double take that was almost comical simply because it was them doing it.

"When did you wake up?" Betty beat Morgan to the punch.

"And what are you doing just walking around?" Morgan added, although I doubted it was less from out of concern and more to do with needing to say something since Betty had.

"I just got up a few minutes ago, and where did Lisa go?" I wasn't going to get into anything with those two right now. I needed to check on my car.

"She went into the garage," another voice chimed in.

Were we just going to break into a Mouseketeer roll call? I peered around the divider that separated my kitchen from the living room. Rain and a few faeries were lounging on my couch passing around a pomegranate. Each would pluck a single bright red seed and pop it into her mouth with a moan of pleasure that was almost pornographic.

I shook my head and went to the garage door. When I opened

it, I was hit by a wave of heat that was almost unbearably hot. It was like the space had been converted into a blast furnace. That could not be good for my car! It would no doubt start peeling the paint and it would wreak havoc on the leather interior.

I stepped into the room that was cast in a deep red light that instantly made me think of lava. There were not two, but rather three of the reddish giants in my garage…but no sign of my car!

"…many times have I told you three that Aoife gets this space from sunset to midnight so that she can sing? You know that if she does not do so every single day, that her voice will deteriorate," Lisa was explaining.

"Like listening to pretty lady sing," one of the male giants said in a voice that reminded me of rocks being ground together.

"I can't sing in this heat!" Aoife reached over Lisa and jabbed a finger at the trio. "How many times do I have to tell you?"

All three dropped their heads like scolded children. And that is when it hit me…they were! Children that is. These three were just youngsters. Holy crap! If they were already this big, what would they grow to be? And how was I going to keep them hidden?

Wait! Why was I already making this my problem? I did not ask for any of it. Only, like it or not…it looked like I was going to have some company for a while. And now I understood Lisa's comment about finding a new house…preferably out in the country.

"You three can either quit channeling, or else get up and leave," Lisa said with motherly authority.

In the blink of an eye, the room went back to normal. Seriously, the temperature plummeted and the red glow vanished.

"Sorry," they grumbled in unison, all of them going so far as to clasp their hands behind their back, look at the floor with pouting expressions, and do that thing where they twist back and forth at the waist just like naughty school children.

With that seemingly handled to everybody's satisfaction, Lisa and I left the garage. I knew there was still a lot of garbage to deal with, and I wanted to get to the bottom of this situation with Lisa, I guess my car could wait…for a few minutes anyway. The basement was obviously not a good place for a private chat.

"My room, now," I said, bee lining for the stairs without waiting to see if she was following. I heard a few people calling my name; a couple were familiar voices, but most were not.

I walked into my room and plopped down on the chair next to my walk-in closet that was almost as big as my old apartment. I was going to miss this room.

Lisa walked in and shut the door behind her. I always knew that she was a smart girl. No doubt she was already prepared for this little confrontation.

I was about to pose my first of what I was figuring to be a few dozen questions when she blurted, "We didn't track down the Templar who was working with Prince Fraylee. Whoever it was got away."

Not actually the question that I had on the tip of my tongue, but I am sure it would have come up. I know that I have a problem with saying the wrong thing sometimes. I don't always think about the words I am about to spew from my mouth or how they may be received.

"How convenient for *you*."

I saw Lisa's expression change very slightly. I was not exactly sure what it was that I was seeing, but I was suddenly remembering every single boyfriend that I had gotten in a fight and broken up with over the years. There is that instant when you know you are passing a point of no return. That voice in your head is screaming for you to shut up, but that head of steam is already sending you careening to that next stop…Spiltsville.

"Do you think that I had something to do with this?" Lisa said in a guarded whisper.

Shut up, Ava, the voice in my head was shouting. *Do that silent thing where you just stare and the person starts blabbing in the uncomfortable hush.* For a moment, I actually thought that it was Adrianna, but I could "feel" her locked securely in the place I had made for her in my mind. However, I was pretty sure I could detect her amusement.

"I don't know what to think anymore when it comes to you," my big mouth said despite the clanging of my internal alarms.

148

"You get buddy-buddy with Morgan and take off to join the Templars—a group that tried to wipe out every single ghoul by the way—and then you hold secret meetings in my house while putting a spell on me that makes me into a freakin' zombie for all intents and purposes. So maybe you tell me what I should be thinking right about now."

"You should be thinking that I am your friend, and that I will always be that above anything else." Lisa turned her head just a little, but I saw her brush at her eyes. She was crying?

One thing I hate is when somebody does you wrong, but then tries to turn the tables and make it seem like you are the bad guy. I know we all do it, but that does not mean that I like it in the slightest when it is done to me. I could sense my feelings start to harden.

That voice in my head was getting the snot kicked out of it. It was growing faint and a new voice that I did not much care for was telling me that I was doing the right thing.

"Friends don't put some sort of mojo on each other. And let's not forget to mention that the secret meetings you were holding in *my* house were with the freakin' Templars! I think I have said it more than once, but it bears repeating. They. Tried. To Kill. Every. Ghoul."

I was in full on bitch mode now. I had even gone so far as to emphasize the word 'my' when mentioning the house. From day one, it had been *ours*. The only thing that was truly mine was the Corvette. Lisa and I were a team…we shared in the risk and the reward. Unfortunately, I was turning a blind eye to all of that. I wish I had a good excuse or reason.

Since this weird little adventure began, I had only one person who stood by me…watched my back…and put up with my quirks. Lisa Jenkins and I had bonded almost like sisters…no…stronger. We were closer than I think I have ever felt or known that it was possible to feel about another person.

So why was I doing this? Why was I tearing this apart? What good did I think was going to come from this?

"There is more going on than either one of us know, Ava," Lisa finally said in a whisper. "And I need you to trust me. I

149

need you to trust that I have your back. I am going to find out what is going on, but for now...I can't tell you anything. I just need you to accept that and trust me."

The golden opportunity to salvage the only really good thing I have in my life was right there. It had been gift wrapped and set before me. All that I had to do was accept it.

"I'm a ghoul. The last thing I can trust is a Templar."

Seriously? Of the billions of word combinations available...those were the ones that I went with?

You are making a mistake, Adrianna's voice chimed as she apparently broke out of whatever brain cell I had her stored in.

I saw the look and knew for certain in the logical part of my mind that I was handling this all wrong. The big problem was my big mouth...and I am not referring to the Sharkmouth version...just the "stupid Ava" version.

How many times have you been there? How many times have you gotten in too deep with your mouth, and now stupid pride or whatever it is that makes you do something or say something really ill-advised to somebody you love and care about won't let you back down...or at least shut the hell up?

"I would never hurt you, Ava." Lisa turned away from me and put her hand on the doorknob. "And, for what it's worth...that will never change. I swear it."

And she walked out, closing the door behind her. I stood there doing my best to build up some indignation. After all, she had been the one sneaking around. She had been the one who put the whammy on me. Right?

I have no idea how long I sat in my room. The first thing I did was focus on locking Adrianna up a little tighter. She kept trying to yammer on about how I needed to "go after the child" and nonsense like that. I was in no mood to hear that kind of talk at the moment.

I was still sitting in the chair and honestly had no idea how much time had passed when a knock came on my door. I debated trying to ignore it, but as soon as I sent my ghoul senses out to find out who it was and came up blank, I already knew.

"What do you want, Morgan?" I growled. This would be a

bad time for her to push my buttons.

"The girl has left," Morgan said as she entered and closed the door behind her. "Is there something that you want to tell me?"

"You never wanted her around anyways," I snapped. "Now she's gone. Happy?"

"Absolutely not." Morgan walked up to me and stood there, just staring. If she was trying to do that thing where she just stares at me and I spill my guts, she was in for a long wait.

Okay...maybe not.

"She is a Templar—" I began, but Morgan cut me off.

"*Studying* to be a Templar," she corrected. "She has quite a ways to go before she is initiated into the organization entirely."

"Sand box...sand trap...cats still poop in them. You are just being technical."

"I am being truthful."

"That would be a first." What the hell; it was out there on the table now. Why not cut it open and see what comes out. "You have withheld information or been just plain deceitful with me since day one. You send me out with no idea what to do and then make it seem like it was all part of this master plan to bring out my ghoulish traits. And then you send Lisa to join the very group that wanted ghouls to go by the way of the unicorn."

"Unicorns are not gone," Morgan said with her usual casual attitude.

"Screw you!"

There was a moment or ten of silence. I wonder if anybody or anything had ever said that to Miss Prissy Pants. Doubtful. But at least it was her that broke the silence this time.

"I sent Lisa to join the Templars for your protection," Morgan finally said with what I was almost sure had to be a hint of emotion in her voice. "There are, currently as far as anybody knows, five ghouls in existence in this world. Considering that they once numbered over a thousand, you can hopefully appreciate your...uniqueness."

I wanted to ask a hundred questions, but I was afraid that she would go back to her old mode of not saying anything. This was a revelation, but I still needed more.

"Lisa is loyal to you in a way that I fail to understand," Morgan continued. She brushed an imaginary wrinkle from my bed and sat on it, putting us basically at eye level. "She would give her life to save yours."

"Did you pick that up while snooping around in her mind?" I asked. Inside I was cursing myself; if I had broken whatever spell had Morgan's tongue suddenly so loose, I would kick my own ass.

Literally.

"I have told you it does not work quite that way. However, I can pick up certain things...especially when they are that strong."

"So why send her to the Templars?"

"Are you—"

She actually clicked her mouth shut. I could see just enough of a twitch in her expression to know that she was ready to snap back with something nasty. After a deep breath that I actually saw and heard, she started over.

"The best way to keep tabs on the enemy is to have somebody in their midst. Your friend Lisa is a much stronger girl than you knew or than I initially realized. Not even their best empath will be able to sense any deception in her. They will believe that she is one of them all the way to the end...should it ever come to that."

I refrained from whipping one hand over my head in a visual display of how much I was grasping. She was talking about things that were just not in my area of comprehension.

"So why couldn't you tell me that from the start?"

"Because I was not entirely sure that she was so strong. By the time I discovered it, we had bigger problems."

That sort of made sense. I mean, we had just averted a possible extinction event or what could have been the end of the entire Supernatural community. When I say that in my head, I'm actually a little impressed with myself. But then another thought hit me out of the blue. It was something that had seemed huge at the moment, but came at the perfectly wrong time.

"Then maybe you can tell me why she has been meeting with

Belinda as well."

If I had not been looking directly at her face I would have missed that tiniest of flickers. She hadn't known! So whatever that was about was something even Little Miss Know-it-all was completely in the dark about. However, in typical Morgan fashion, she underestimated me and answered like I hadn't seen what I was certain to be a look of total surprise flash across her face.

"That is their business, and I leave it to them to make known to you what they choose."

"Should I go after her?" That seemed like a logical question, and one that I figured would give me that rare direct answer.

"You must decide that for yourself, Ava." Morgan rose and walked to the door. "But I have a feeling that there are some far stranger things ahead. Perhaps it would be better for you to be free of distractions."

"Lisa wasn't a distraction," I said with surprisingly less anger than I felt. "Lisa was...is...Lisa *is* my friend."

"Then perhaps you would be doing her a favor by leaving her be...at least for the immediate future."

And just like that, she was the Morgan I had always known. She set an envelope on my dresser and said nothing more as she walked out the door.

I was at a loss. Maybe she was right. If Lisa went on her way and spent some time with the Templars, perhaps she would be able to protect herself from whatever else lay ahead of us. Only, I was afraid that maybe she would decide that she didn't want to ever come back.

You know that ridiculous saying that people use about setting something free...and if it comes back? Well I always thought that was one of the stupidest things in the world. I believe that, if you love something, you do everything in your power (with the exception of going to the extremes that crazy lady did in *Misery*) to keep it in your life.

More Titles From May December Publications

The Ava Series by TW Brown

That Ghoul Ava: Her First Adventures
That Ghoul Ava and The Queen of the Zombies

The Dead Series by TW Brown

Dead:The Ugly Beginning book 1
Dead: Revelations book 2
Dead: Fortunes and Failures book 3
Dead: Winter book 4
Dead: Siege and Survival book 5
Dead: Confrontation book 6
Dead: Reborn book 7

The Fervor Series by Chantal Boudreau

Fervor book 1
Elevation book 2
Transcendence book 3
Providence book 4

The Highway to Hell Series by Alex Laybourne

Highway to Hell book 1
Trials and Tribulations book 2

The Immortal War Series by Suzi M

Nemesis book 1
Lamia book 2
The Tower book 3 coming soon

The Master's & Renegades Series by Chantal Boudreau

Magic University book 1
Casualties of War book 2
Prisoner of Fate book 3

The Monster Squad Series by Heath Stallcup

Return of the Phoenix book 1
Full Moon Rising book 2

The Zomblog Series by TW Brown

Zomblog book 1
Zomblog II book 2
Zomblog The Final Entry book 3
Zomblog: Snoe book 4
Zomblog: Snoe's War book 5
Zomblog: Snoe's Journey book 6

Special Editions by TW Brown

DEAD: The Geeks
DEAD: Vignettes
DEAD:Steve's Story
DEAD: Special Edition Compendium 1
DEAD: The Geeks 2
DEAD: Vignettes 2
DEAD:Steve's Story 2
DEAD: Special Edition Compendium 2
Zomblog: Compendium 1

Stand Alone Titles

Agape by Bennie Newsome
Cryptic by DA Chaney
Dakota by Todd Brown
Dead Men Tell No Tales by Jeffrey Kosh
Elena by Duncan Lloyd
Eat Wild, Eat Healthy, Eat Green by Donna Johnson
Five by Jeffrey Kosh
Goddesses of Lilith by Tracy Ford
Gruesomely Grimm Zombie Tales -1 by TW Brown
In The Arms of Nightmares by Robert Dean
Legacy of the Dead by RD Teun
Stories Around the Campfire with Uncle Eric by Eric Pollarine
The BoogeyMann by Bennie Newsome
The Book of Joseph by Erik Rise
The Exoterrestrials by TW Brown
The Post-Apacolyptic Cookbook by Donna Johnson
Whisper to a Scream by PS Turner

Anthologies

A Clockworks Orchard: Rivets & Rain
Chivalry is Dead – all male authors
Dear Santa

You can find our titles on Audio as well.

Find them on Audible.com

MAY DECEMBER
Publications

**The growing voice in horror
and speculative fiction.**

Find us at www.maydecemberpublications.com
Or
Email us at contact@maydecemberpublications.com

His blog can be found at:http://twbrown.blogspot.com

The best way to find everything he has out is to start at his Amazon Author Page:http://www.amazon.com/TW-Brown/e/B00363NQI6

You can follow him on twitter @maydecpub and on Facebook under Todd Brown, Author TW Brown, and also under May December Publications.

TW Brown is the author of the ***Zomblog*** series, his horror comedy romp, ***That Ghoul Ava***, and, of course...the ***DEAD*** series. Safely tucked away in the beautiful Pacific Northwest, he moves away from his desk only at the urging of his Border Collie, Aoife. (Pronounced Eye-fa)

He plays a little guitar on the side...just for fun...and makes up any excuse to either go trail hiking or strolling along his favorite place...Cannon Beach. He answers all his emails sent to twbrown.maydecpub @gmail.com and tries to thank everybody personally when they take the time to leave a review of one of his works.